"This mission could be deadly if you don't know what you're doing, Solange. Tell me now if you aren't sure, and I'll get you out of here."

Jack's hand on her arm gripped with increased intensity. Solange realized he was afraid for her. Really afraid, to the point where he might abandon the mission if she seemed reluctant.

"I know what to do," she assured him, putting more conviction into her answer than she truly felt.

In a surprising move, he put his arms around her and held her close. "I wish to God I had left you where you were. You're not cut out for this."

She pushed against his chest until she could look him straight in the eye. "Don't underestimate me, Mercier."

He smiled down at her, still holding her in his arms. "My mistake." Then he lowered his head and kissed her.

Solange felt it to her soul.

Dear Reader,

Once again, Silhouette Intimate Moments has a month's worth of fabulous reading for you. Start by picking up *Wanted,* the second in Ruth Langan's suspenseful DEVIL'S COVE miniseries. This small town is full of secrets, and this top-selling author knows how to keep readers turning the pages.

We have more terrific miniseries. Kathleen Creighton continues STARRS OF THE WEST with *An Order of Protection,* featuring a protective hero every reader will want to have on her side. In *Joint Forces,* Catherine Mann continues WINGMEN WARRIORS with Tag's long-awaited story. Seems Tag and his wife are also awaiting something: the unexpected arrival of another child. Carla Cassidy takes us back to CHEROKEE CORNERS in *Manhunt.* There's a serial killer on the loose, and only the heroine's visions can help catch him—but will she be in time to save the hero? *Against the Wall* is the next SPECIAL OPS title from Lyn Stone, a welcome addition to the line when she's not also writing for Harlequin Historicals. Finally, you knew her as Anne Avery, also in Harlequin Historicals, but now she's Anne Woodard, and in *Dead Aim* she proves she knows just what contemporary readers want.

Enjoy them all—and come back next month, when Silhouette Intimate Moments brings you even more of the best and most exciting romance reading around.

Yours,

Leslie J. Wainger
Executive Editor

Please address questions and book requests to:
Silhouette Reader Service
U.S.: 3010 Walden Ave., P.O. Box 1325, Buffalo, NY 14269
Canadian: P.O. Box 609, Fort Erie, Ont. L2A 5X3

Against the Wall
LYN STONE

Silhouette®

INTIMATE MOMENTS™

Published by Silhouette Books

America's Publisher of Contemporary Romance

SILHOUETTE BOOKS

ISBN 0-373-27365-7

AGAINST THE WALL

Copyright © 2004 by Lynda Stone

Visit Silhouette Books at www.eHarlequin.com

Printed in U.S.A.

LYN STONE

loves creating pictures with words. Paints, too. Her love affair with writing and art began in the third grade, when she won a school-wide prize for her colorful poster for Book Week. She spent the prize money on books, one of which was *Little Women*.

She rewrote the ending so that Jo marries her childhood sweetheart. That's because Lyn had a childhood sweetheart herself and wanted to marry him when she grew up. She did. And now she is living her "happily ever after" in north Alabama with the same guy. She and Allen have traveled the world, have two children, four grandchildren and experienced some wild adventures along the way.

Whether writing romantic historicals or contemporary fiction, Lyn insists on including elements of humor, mystery and danger. Perhaps because that other book she purchased all those years ago was a *Nancy Drew*.

This book is dedicated to
retired Special Agent Frank Hudson, Dorothy and Jim.
We miss you guys!

Prologue

"I don't see how we're gonna be much help to Jack fifteen clicks away," Joe Corda said. He immediately lowered his voice when he heard the echo bounce off the old masonry walls. "That's lethal stuff he'll be dealing with. Not like bullets. One hit and he's dead. If he were going in alone, I wouldn't worry so much, but he'll have that doctor along. And the kid."

"He'll need tickets and they're it. I'd have gotten us closer, but we'd stick out like M&Ms on a sushi plate anywhere else around here," Holly Amberson argued. "As it is, the locals won't even blink at us. They're used to weirdos renting this place. *Artistes!*" she hissed with a flourish of her fingers.

He looked around as he put down two of the suitcases. "This dump looks like something out of a really bad French novel."

"Oh, yeah, like you've read so many of *those*," she

muttered. "But I will admit a Bela Lugosi butler wouldn't be out of place."

He leveled her with a look. "*We* are the help, remember?"

"Not you, slick." She smirked. "You are the gigolo. Man, I do hate that shirt. Which pimp's closet did you raid anyway?"

Just outside, Martine Duquesne Corda was busy issuing imperious instructions to her bodyguard, Eric Vinland, and chauffeur, Will Griffin. Holly laughed. "Martine's really getting into her role. You let her boss *you* around like that?"

"Sure." Joe shrugged, hands on his hips, preoccupied with taking in the rustic, old-world charm of the faded mansion in France's Lorraine region. "She does have an image to maintain. How do you like her disguise? She'll be just that beautiful when she does reach sixty, I bet."

In an abrupt change of topic, Holly commented, "Where the heck are the outlets in this barn? I need a place to hook up." She hefted the case containing assorted gadgets and her laptop and set it on a scarred marble-topped table near the door.

They both moved aside as the others entered. She waited until Will had closed the door. "All the rooms been swept?"

"Clean," Eric assured her. "We're good to go." He turned to Martine, clicked his heels and bowed, looking more like a muscle-bound kid on spring break than the bodyguard he was supposed to be. "Our reclusive Madame D'Amato may proceed with her work uninhibited." He peered over his wire-rimmed glasses and winked at Joe. "As well as her play, of course." Caught off guard, Martine laughed and blushed.

Holly pointed to the mound of luggage now piled near their feet. "You guys cut the bull and set up the global positioning system. Let's check Jack's location. We need to know exactly when to expect him."

Will, quintessential agent, the quiet man, finally spoke. "His ETA's eleven-thirty, give or take five. He'll be here."

"Verify." Holly was running this end of the mission. Joe reached for the case with the GPS instruments. His duties consisted of whatever Holly ordered him to do. And also protecting his wife, not an official member of the Sextant team but a contract language specialist who was central to their cover. Holly, Will, Eric and he were masquerading as her entourage. Clay Senate was maintaining Stateside control while the boss, Mercier, had assumed the lead.

The Sextant team consisted of agents recruited from various government organizations expressly for the purpose of preventing terrorist activities around the globe. This suspected bio-terror threat was the first of its kind for Sextant.

Identify, Infiltrate, Analyze and Eliminate. That first part, they had all had a hand in. The second and most difficult order of business was about to go down within the next few hours if all went as planned. The primary agent was about to insert.

Joe looked up at the peeling paint on the fancy plaster ceiling and—seriously lapsed Catholic that he was— uttered a devout prayer that they would all survive. He was known for his hunches, and he had a really bad feeling about this.

Chapter 1

Jack Mercier entered the hospital wing of Baumettes Prison with the barrel of a submachine gun resting at the base of his spine. While he loved humanity—in fact, had devoted his life to the protection of it—he had decided since coming to this place a week ago that he was not that crazy about people. Especially Claude Bujold, his least favorite guard.

Maybe he was rationalizing the fact that he wanted to kill the man, but he didn't think so. Claude considered beatings a form of entertainment, the more helpless the victim, the greater the rush. Misuse of power really pushed Jack's buttons.

Jack was supposed to be awaiting arraignment, accused of conspiring to ship illegal weapons into France. Bogus charges, of course, faked to get him into this place.

He had escaped most of the vicious harassment by bribing Claude. The promise of money from Jack's attorney had gotten Jack the promise of medical attention today.

Jack waited until they entered the small ward, empty now except for one patient and the doctor attending him at the far end of the room. Today was the day.

The white-clad doctor who was bending over the patient stood and turned. Jack stopped in his tracks. *Wrong doctor. Most definitely, wrong doctor.*

Should he postpone? Too late. With everything else in place, it was now or never.

Claude prodded him down the aisle between the rows of beds. "Hey, Doc, this piece of filth has been complaining of chest pain. Would you—"

Jack whirled, grasped both of Claude's wrists and pinched the nerves that controlled his fingers. He rammed the top of his head beneath Claude's chin and heard a satisfying crack.

The machine gun fell, hitting the floor a split second after Jack's knee connected with Claude's groin.

The guard crumpled with a cry. Jack delivered a blow to the side of the head that would keep Claude unconscious for a while. Unfortunately, the bastard had to be left alive.

The doctor rushed him but he heard that coming. He waited, caught her upraised arm and easily removed the syringe, her impromptu weapon.

"Where is Dr. Micheaux?" he demanded.

She sputtered as she struggled to break free. Her small fists bounced off him, inflicting no pain. She was not very strong, he noted.

What the hell was this delicate little flower doing in a prison hospital? And what had happened to the doctor he had expected to find in here?

Now he would either have to incapacitate her like the

guard, or take her along. Either way, she might be blamed for aiding the escape. Besides, he had to have a doctor along. She'd just have to do.

"Be still or I'll have to kill you," he snapped.

All motion ceased. Her wide blue gaze, full of fear and anger, settled on his. Every muscle in her body was alert and tensed for further action if he presented her a chance. Bold little thing.

"I admire bravery but not stupidity. Nod if you comprehend." He spoke to her in French, assuming that she was.

Her chin remained raised, her glare defiant. But Jack could see she understood. She was pretty, he noticed. Blond, sky-blue eyes, skin untouched by the sun. This one didn't spend her off days on the Riviera, that was for sure. Too busy saving lives, he guessed. He'd bet she worked here for nothing in her spare time. Talk about being in the wrong place at the wrong time.

"Prepare your patient to leave the prison. Is he ambulatory?"

"No," she said emphatically. "You are not taking him anywhere."

Jack inclined his head toward the exit that led to the alley where a truck was waiting. "We are all leaving through that door in less than five minutes." He glared at her. He had no time for her spitfire attitude, so he added, "Dead or alive. Your choice, lady."

For a long moment she studied his eyes, then looked back at the bed where her patient lay sleeping. "You won't hurt him?"

"No. Or you, either. Not if you behave and do exactly as I tell you."

She exhaled the pent-up breath she was holding and nodded once, no doubt cursing the abominable lack of security in French prisons. This one was even more short-handed than usual today thanks to Will Griffin.

Jack released her and reached down to pick up Claude's weapon. "Get to it, then, while I take care of the garbage. Do as I say and neither of you will be harmed. My word."

He ignored her scoff. In seconds he had bound the unconscious Claude's hands and feet and gagged him with a roll of gauze.

Jack regretted having to take the doctor along, but he really had no choice. Since the boy was drugged, some-one would have to verify how he'd been rescued. Be-sides that, he obviously needed medical attention, and the kid's father would hardly appreciate Jack's getting the boy out of prison if the little fellow died in the process.

"You have the boy ready?" Jack demanded as he approached the sickbed where the prisoner lay.

"Yes. Why are you doing this?" she demanded.

Jack ignored the question. "Take as much of his medication as you have with you. Hand me your bag."

"I am not coming," she informed him.

"Poor choice." He started raising the machine gun. She gasped.

"Change your mind?" Jack asked. Again she nod-ded, her eyes clenched in resignation.

"Then help him up. He's small enough you should be able to manage. Is he really that hurt or just se-dated?"

"Of course he is hurt. His injuries are numerous and he is on morphine."

As she spoke, she raised the boy to a sitting position, eased his legs off the bed and tried to encourage him to stand up. She managed, but only just. The kid was pretty much out of it. He was very slightly built, almost delicate. Though he was seventeen, René Chari seemed younger. His sallow complexion and adolescent fuzz of a mustache only enhanced his look of vulnerability.

"Brace your shoulder beneath his and pull his arm around your neck," Jack told her, grasping the boy beneath his other arm as they shuffled him to the door. "We have only a short way to go."

"This door is kept locked," she told him.

"Not today," Jack replied as he reached for the handle and shoved the door open. "Go ahead of me. And if you run, I *will* shoot."

She did as ordered and they were soon in the alley. No windows graced the inner walls that faced them between the wings. A heavy chain-link gate topped with concertina wire barred the only way out. "Hurry. Let's get him inside the vehicle."

The truck provided, a megaton monstrosity used for delivering supplies, would easily roll them to freedom. Several blocks away, a vintage sedan waited, souped up and ready to transport them to their eventual destination.

He placed the machine gun across his lap, cranked the starter, floored the accelerator and gunned it, ramming straight through the chain-link barrier.

The alarm was immediate and deafening. He sped away from it, taking side streets until he approached the wooded area of the park.

He pulled up behind the car Griffin had left him and slammed on the brake. In minutes he had loaded both patient and doctor into the gray Saab and they were off.

"Jail break accomplished," he said to himself, ticking off tasks to be completed. It was an old habit. He turned to the doctor who looked pale as a bleached sheet. "Are you doing all right?"

She shot him a look of disbelief that he would ask such a ridiculous question. "I have been abducted at gunpoint. No, I am not well at all." She swallowed hard, almost gulped. "Do you mean to...kill me?" she added, still defiant.

Her bravery, useless as it was, touched something in Jack. She was so totally defenseless and yet she refused to cower. A kitten backed against a wall, facing a bulldog, ready to claw for all she was worth if attacked. He felt faintly ashamed of himself. "Did I hurt you when I disarmed you?"

She flexed her wrist. Faint red marks discolored the pale ivory of her flesh where he had grasped it to relieve her of the syringe. She tucked that hand beneath the other and began rubbing the wrist slowly, absently. "No, but you did not answer my question."

"I have no plans at present to harm you at all if you cooperate. You've not asked me once to release you since we escaped. Why is that?"

Her gaze left him as she glanced into the back seat. "There is René. He needs continued care and I doubt you intend to give it. What do you plan to do with him?"

"Take him home to his father," Jack told her. "What happened to Dr. Micheaux?"

"I *am* Dr. Micheaux," she replied with a haughty look. "Solange Micheaux."

Damn. The daughter of the other doctor. He remembered a mention of her in Micheaux's dossier, but *nothing* about her working at Baumettes. "Where is your father today?"

She refused to answer.

"He was supposed to be there and had promised to

help," Jack said, hoping that might gain him a little cooperation.

"You lie! My father would never assist in such a thing."

"This is more than a run-of-the-mill escape, Doctor. Now where is your father?"

Her frown deepened, and she remained silent for a minute before answering. "In Paris."

"Why wasn't he at the prison today?"

She sighed. "He is in Broussais Hospital. He was injured in an accident yesterday morning."

Either the team had not heard anything about this development or hadn't been able to get word of it to him in his cell. "What happened?" Jack asked. "And are you certain it was an accident?

He heard her swift intake of breath. "He…he was hit by an automobile as he crossed the street. You…you are saying it was not an accident?"

"No. It probably was," Jack said, but he was far from sure of the answer. "How badly was he hurt?"

She glanced out the window and continued to rub her hands together. "Broken femur, a concussion, bruises. He will recover." Then she faced Jack, her eyes imploring. "Let me go to him. We can take René there, as well. You could leave us at the emergency entrance and be well away in no time. I promise—"

"Save your breath," he said, interrupting her. "That's not going to happen. I have to get René to his father no later than tomorrow. Do you know where he lives? Has the boy told you?"

"You do not even know where you are to go?"

Jack almost laughed. "Of course I know. I need to know if *you* know already. If René has said anything at all to you about his home or his family."

She sighed, then looked out the window at the passing scenery. "No. René has not been living with his father. The boy has rooms near the Sorbonne where he attends classes," she muttered, as if to herself.

Jack nodded. "Art student. Has he talked about his family? His father in particular?"

"Not to me and Father did not mention his discussing anything of that nature." Her interest in the passing landscape ended abruptly as she turned that electrifying blue gaze on him again. "Why all of these questions?"

"I'll tell you later. What of you, Dr. Micheaux? Will you tell me about yourself?"

"Why should I?"

"Because I ask."

She scoffed. "You already know my name and who my father is. Even that is too much."

"I am Jacques Mercier. Now you know mine. I was imprisoned to await trial. Wouldn't you like to know why?"

"No. It is nothing to do with me. Are you attempting to cultivate the Stockholm Syndrome with this foolish exchange of information? I promise you I will never become attached to an abductor no matter how friendly you try to be."

She faced away from him again. "Stop looking at me that way."

Jack hadn't realized he was making her even more uncomfortable. It would be difficult not to look at her. She was something to see, that was for sure.

He should try to put her at ease, as much as he could. "You're very brave, that much I already know. Instead of a mere profession, you have a calling, I believe. Anyone else would be begging me for their freedom. Instead, you are willing to go along to care for our young friend in the back seat. Are you afraid?'' He knew she was terrified, but he also knew she would never admit it.

"Of course I am afraid," she confessed, surprising him. "Only a fool would not fear you. I saw what you did to that guard."

"I could easily have killed him," Jack said in a slightly defensive tone.

"I know," she replied, not quite hiding a shiver.

He could see that that thought relieved her only a little. "You need not worry about rape, either," he told her. "I believe I can restrain my animal instincts."

She tried to cover her relief with a mirthless laugh. "I have offended you by thinking you might?"

"Do you care whether I am offended?"

She didn't bother to answer. Jack knew she cared. She had to worry if she had made him angry, that he might change his mind and show her who was boss here.

"You're safe with me," he said, and meant it, too. Not just about his leaving her alone physically. He felt a need to protect her, even from the worry she must be feeling at the moment.

For an instant he considered stopping the car in the next village they reached and letting her go. Bad idea, and he couldn't imagine why he had even thought of doing it. There was the mission to consider, and she was crucial to the success of it. Without her help, the plan would fall apart before it got underway.

That had been the point of waiting until the doctor was with the boy to take him. The problem was that her father had eagerly agreed to help with this. The man had experience in this sort of enterprise, had worked

with intelligence before. The daughter had no clue what
was going on.

"We'll have to lie low for a day," he said, knowing
she would assume the police would be giving chase.
There would be no all-points bulletin on them, of
course. Holly Amberson could take care of that with a
few choice phone calls and a bit of hacking with her
magic laptop.

"Open the glove compartment and get the phone,"
he commanded.

After eyeing him with suspicion for a few seconds,
she complied. He took it from her before she could
punch in any numbers and pressed the precoded digit.

When Holly answered, he kept his message brief and
to the point. "We have a substitute. See that Dr. *Solange* Micheaux is officially listed on emergency leave.
Arrange for someone to handle her duties and cover for
her. Her father is an accident victim, a patient at Broussais. Check on his condition." He paused. "And make
sure it really was an accident."

Amberson did not waste words either. "So we are
still on?"

"Unless the mission is compromised. Are things all
set at your end?"

"Right on schedule," she replied.

That meant word would soon be out that the son of
Ahmed Chari had escaped Baumettes Prison with a little
help from a fellow inmate. This way, Chari probably
would not be surprised by his son's arrival if he heard
about the escape on the news. The police would not
bother to question Chari. They would be informed there
was evidence that his son and his accomplices had left
the country immediately.

Jack would use the downtime to become better acquainted with the doctor and determine whether she could be trusted with the truth or if she should go in blind.

Taking her in her father's stead bothered him. It shouldn't. She was just one person, expendable in the big scheme of things. The big scheme here was to save lives. Many of them. If sacrifices were necessary to accomplish that, then he would just have to live with it.

Solange realized she had dozed when the car stopped. She ran her hands through her hair and shook off her grogginess. How on earth had she managed to fall sleep in such a predicament as this?

Before she fell asleep, she had been marking their route visually. They had headed north from Lyon, with the central highlands to their left and the Swiss Alps to their right. Vineyards and fruit orchards lined their way along the wide path cut by nature.

When she looked out now, there were no landmarks or identifying characteristics on the eerie, moonlit landscape. He might have changed direction entirely. They could be anywhere in France by now.

"We'll stay here for the night."

She looked at the man who had kidnapped her, then out the window again. "Would you tell me where we are?"

"A safe place," he replied cryptically.

He got out, opened the back door and gently lifted René in his arms. Solange hopped out quickly and hovered, cautioning him to be careful not to jostle her patient any more than he could help.

The night was chilly for mid-May, but that was not what caused her to shiver. She rubbed her arms briskly.

"Look under the mat there and find the key," he ordered, his voice curt.

She hurried to find it and unlock the door to the old house, feeling for the keyhole with trembling fingers. What would happen once they were inside?

Where was this place? The moon was high enough that she could see they were not in a town or village. In fact, she could see no other buildings except this old cottage they were entering.

Could this man be intending to hold René here for ransom? And, if so, what would happen to her? If René remained unconscious during all this, he could not identify his kidnapper. But she could. Perhaps she would live only so long as René needed her.

If she found an opportunity, she would escape. Then she could go to the police and have them rescue René.

"There should be an oil lamp and matches on the table. Careful you don't knock it off and break it," he said, moving farther into the main room.

She heard the rustle of movement as she discovered by feel the lamp and a box of matches where he had said they would be. She struck fire and lifted the old-fashioned globe.

When she had adjusted the flame, Solange carried it over to where he had laid René on a shabby, but comfortable-looking couch.

"See to him. I'll go and get your medical bag," Mercier told her.

"Is there water in here or must we go outside to draw it?" she asked.

"Running water. The bath is off the hallway. Kitchen's through that door," he said pointing.

She knelt beside the couch and began checking René's pulse. It felt steady and strong enough. He breathed normally and seemed to be quite comfortable. She lifted his lids and examined his pupils in the lamp light. A crocheted afghan lay draped over the foot of the couch and she used that to cover him against the chill of the room.

Mercier returned quickly and handed her the bag. "How is he doing?"

"No worse than he was."

"His pain was severe enough for morphine?"

She hesitated. "First answer me one thing. Are you holding René for ransom?"

"No," he declared shaking his head. Then he seemed to think about it. "But I can see why you might think that's what I'm doing. No, I'm returning him to his father as soon as I can. I was escaping, anyway, and thought I might as well take the boy out of there with me."

"On the hope of a reward, perhaps?" she asked.

He shrugged. "That and a place to hide once I got out. I'm hoping Chari will offer me a job."

"You said my father agreed to help you? Why?"

"Even before he was beaten, the boy was not strong enough to survive long where he was. Your father knew that, and I suspect you know it, too."

Satisfied he was not lying, she answered his question truthfully. "René was hurt, yes. He could have borne it well enough with pills, but my father wanted him bedridden, to seem worse off than he was."

Mercier's dark eyes softened as he crouched beside her on the threadbare rug. "To protect him? So he wouldn't have to return to the cells?"

She nodded. "He has been at the prison for over three weeks and this is his second beating. That is why Father gave him morphine. If René remained unconscious, he would have more time to heal. When my father told me of his condition, both of us tried to intervene on René's behalf, plead his youth and size to someone in authority. But neither my father nor I could get in to see anyone in the prefecture or the warden's office. Even if we had, they probably would have laughed at us. He is simply another prisoner to be locked away. Why should they care?''

''But you care.''

''Of course I care!'' she exclaimed, glaring at him. ''He is hardly more than a child. Look at him. A gentle boy. How could they put him in with all those monsters?'' Oh God, what had she said? She had just included this man in that insult.

But instead of outrage, she saw full understanding in his eyes. ''Good for you. Your father and you outwitted them.'' He smiled at her then, a gentle expression she would not have expected from such a man.

''We do what we can, though it is never enough.''

He nodded. ''Baumettes is a three-hour drive down from Paris. Do you come to work at the prison hospital often?''

''Whenever my schedule permits, I assist my father in his volunteer work. Since his retirement, he spends a good many hours at three of the prison facilities.'' She could see no point in going into their reasons for doing what they did.

He sighed. It was more a gust of resigned frustration. ''One of my people is checking on your father's condition and you'll be advised how he is tomorrow. Try not to worry about him, though I'm certain you will, anyway.''

''Then I must thank you for that, I suppose.'' Solange

slumped, burying her face in her hands. She felt like weeping but knew she must not.

She took a deep breath and raised her head again, meeting his eyes. "I am very tired. Would you mind if I lie here on the floor beside the divan and sleep for a while? I had duty in the emergency last night and was unable to rest."

He straightened and held up one finger. "Wait just a minute."

Before she knew it, he was dragging in a single-bed mattress. "Here you are," he said, positioning it next to her. "I'm afraid there are no linens. But here is a pillow and it's new."

She took the pillow from him and lay down.

Her captor offered her a reassuring smile and went to sit on the floor beside the front door. Somehow she knew that was the only exit that she would be able open.

It would be useless effort to try to escape tonight. He would only come after her, and she had no idea which way she should run even if he did not bother. Perhaps tomorrow would afford her a chance.

It was more than she could manage to stay awake and worry or react to any leftover fear. She would simply have to trust the angels as her mother used to say.

In the dream that followed close on the heels of her surrender to sleep, Solange felt one of them brush a wing over her face to comfort her. It rested lightly on her head for a long moment, a blessing, a promise to ward off evil. She smiled and felt safe.

Chapter 2

Jack stirred the bacon, careful to do it precisely as Holly had once shown him. He was not much of a cook but had been trying to learn. Since Holly was the only woman who worked with him and the only person he knew who didn't exist on junk food and the occasional outing at a restaurant, she had volunteered.

Holly was slipping in under his guard, and he would have to watch that. Nothing sexual going on, but he was damn close to regarding her as a friend, not just one of the team.

Come to think of it, he had been spending a little too much of his free time with the others, too. Camaraderie was one thing; getting to be buddies was quite another. Maybe this mission would put things back in perspective.

He liked field work, but missed the daily routine in the office. Sometimes he could pretend for days he was just an average nine-to-fiver, fighting the traffic to work where he'd spend all day arranging investments and contacting clients. Visit his parents when it proved convenient. Maybe meet some interesting female for drinks after hours once in a while, get it on later if she seemed interested.

That was his life for about two weeks out of twelve. The rest of the time he was checking out rumors of terrorist rumblings and trying to stamp out trouble before it got underway. So far they had been successful beyond their best expectations going into this.

He thought about the woman in the next room, the pretty little doctor who had inadvertently become involved in this mission. Solange Micheaux was the least likely person he could imagine for getting wound up in any intrigue. What an open book. No guile whatsoever. She was so totally unlike the women engaged in this business, she could blow the whole op and ruin everything.

He pretty much lived for his job now, that of SAIC, or Special Agent in Charge, of a fairly new team called SEXTANT, consisting of six specialists recruited from different U.S. Government agencies. Organizations that had previously spent a great deal of their time bickering over jurisdiction and jealously guarding from each other the info they dug up. With the team's respective contacts within their old jobs, and full allegiance to the new one, intelligence had a fighting chance of getting combined and doing some good.

Jack was formerly with the National Security Agency, the NSA, fondly dubbed No Such Agency because of its covert nature. The others were from the FBI, DIA, CIA, DEA and ATF.

They all had their own specialties, though they usually teamed up to make use of unique talents. As a rule,

only one actually went in undercover. That depended
on who was most suited for the job. In this instance,
Jack's French was best, learned at his mother's knee
instead of books or tapes. So was his ability to resolve
matters without the use of weapons.

Jack had handpicked the agents on his team. He ad-
mittedly chose several of them for their psychic abilities. Paranormal gifts had always fascinated him. While
these talents weren't officially listed on their résumés,
their extrasensory perceptions had been extremely help-
ful so far.

Jack wished he possessed a little mind-reading ca-
pability right now so he could decide whether Dr. Micheaux would become a help or a hindrance.

He stirred the bacon some more, then flopped it onto
the waiting plates. The eggs were going to be a problem. He always had trouble with eggs.

"What are you doing?"

He eyed the eggs again, reluctant to turn around and
face her. She would look soft and deliciously rumpled,
he knew. She even sounded that way. Damn, she was
attractive. And very distracting.

What was she doing to him? He had to get a grip.
Must be her French, that faint Parisian-born drawl like
none other, he guessed. Could be she reminded him of
his mother a little. She sounded a bit like her. She even
had that little one-shoulder shrug he remembered his
mother using. Only on Solange, it looked a damn sight
more interesting.

"I'm making breakfast," he answered, his words a
little more gruff than he intended. No, it was not Mama
he was thinking about at the moment. Not even close.

She brushed past him and reached for the coffeepot
sitting on the stove and poured herself a cup. When her

arm touched his, he nearly jumped, catching himself
just in time. He wasn't exactly Mr. Cool this morning,
he thought with a grimace.

Jack kept doing what he was doing, shoring up his
internal defenses, cracking eggs and trying to concentrate on how Holly had taught him to do that one-
handed. He nearly crushed the first one and stifled a
curse.

"Move out of the way," Solange ordered and took
the bowl of eggs and fork out of his hand.

He watched the impatient little shake of her head as
she took over. In no time she had turned out a perfect,
fluffy omelette, which she neatly halved and slid onto
the two plates he'd put out on the table.

Then she sat across from him and they ate, wordlessly
eyeing each other in the way two strangers might do
who had shared a night together and could find nothing
to say when morning came.

Essentially that's what they were, he supposed. There
was even a faint sexual undertone present, though he
had scarcely touched her at all and never with that intent. He wanted to, however, and that was the problem.
She couldn't know that, of course. And definitely
wouldn't share the feeling or appreciate his telling her
about his. When they had finished eating, she gathered
up the dishes and began to wash up.

He knew he had to gain her trust, and so far he hadn't
done much in the way of accomplishing that. He also
decided he would trust her. Maybe it was the tender
way she treated the boy and how she had leaped to his
defense. There was a goodness about Solange Micheaux
that seemed to emanate from her pores like a sweet
fresh scent.

"Would you leave that and sit down again?" he asked politely. "We need to talk."

Immediately she dried her hands on a towel and complied. Why wouldn't she? He was her captor, or at least she thought of him that way.

She leveled a questioning look at him but didn't speak.

"There is something I need to explain to you." Still, Jack hesitated and looked through the doorway at René Chari. "Are you certain he's still unconscious?"

"He is asleep."

"Would you check on him and see if he's conscious?"

"I did before I came in and he is not. His vitals are acceptable under the circumstances. I expect he will recover completely, but not anytime soon."

"My point is, are you certain he can't overhear what I'm about to tell you?"

"Why?" She frowned, and the expression tugged at him, made him want to erase it and put a smile there. He had not seen her smile and imagined it would be like sunlight on water.

Jack shook off the thought that was a little too poetic for comfort. "Just tell me if there's any chance he's awake right now."

"None. I doubt he will awaken for hours."

Jack relaxed a bit. He needed to bring her in on the plan. She would be able to sink him with a word when they encountered Chari, but he was literally betting his life that she wouldn't. "I have to trust you," he told her. "May I call you Solange?"

"No, you may not. Are you going to explain now why are you doing this?"

"Yes, Doctor, I'm getting to that if you'll give me a

chance.'' He took a deep breath and made the plunge. ''I work for the government.''

Her blue eyes narrowed with suspicion. ''Which government?''

''Yours and mine in this instance. I am an American.''

''Well, that explains much. Are you annexing France or what?''

Jack smiled at the jab. ''Not right now. We received intelligence about a month ago that a man called Ahmed Chari has set up a laboratory where he's concocting a deadly virus that he intends to sell for use as a biological weapon.''

She gasped, covering her mouth with the fingertips of one hand. ''No!''

''Yes. There's a possibility that he plans to test it here. If he sells it to the groups that will want it most, Americans everywhere will be at risk. It's possible he's only a puppet for some larger power that could be using him and others like him to establish a supply of bioweapons. We have to find out.''

''But...but this is terrible!''

''And unfortunately, true.''

''Who told you this?''

She had trouble believing it. It did sound far-fetched unless you dealt with these monsters on a regular basis and knew what they were capable of. ''Someone with inside information. Unfortunately not enough information. What he related about the supplies Chari had purchased for that purpose proved to be true. Your intelligence people have been performing surveillance, and two agents have attempted to infiltrate. They haven't been seen since. I need to work my way into his operation and see how far he's been able to take it. And what else or who else might be involved.''

''Why not simply go in by force and arrest this man?'' she asked.

''I told you. We need to know whether he is working independently or if his setup is but one of a number of labs doing this. Also, we have to find out who is to receive his product, where they are located and, of course, their affiliation.''

''If you have him in custody, surely you could force him to reveal all of this.''

''Torture?'' he asked. ''We have to suppose he would never talk, even on pain of death. If he is a fanatic, he would fight to the death. Or kill himself as we go in. If he is just a supplier with no ideological motive, he and those working for him would be more afraid of his clients than of us. These people use families as leverage. As you must know, truth serum's vastly overrated. So, we have to extract the information, all of it, by other means. In this case, by gaining his trust if we can.''

''And after you do?'' she asked breathlessly.

''Perform what damage control we can, destroy the product and put him out of business permanently.''

''Kill him?'' she asked in a broken whisper.

''Yes, if necessary,'' Jack replied. ''At least lock him away where he'll present no further threat.''

''I do not believe you. This is not real.'' But he could hear the horror in her voice. She didn't dare *not* believe him and they both knew it.

''We had planned for your father to go in with me when we reach Chari's chateau,'' he told her. ''Someone would need to explain how I managed to get René out of Baumettes. The boy cannot do that, since he was drugged and unaware. I want Chari to hire me to work for him out of gratitude.''

"How can you trust he will do that? Do you know anything about this man?'' she asked, hitting squarely on his main problem.

"Not as much as I would like. If you go in with me to verify details of the escape, you will probably be confined once we arrive, kept only to minister to Chari's son, until we have this resolved. It shouldn't take long. All you would need to do is keep the boy sedated and comfortable and stay where they put you. It's highly unlikely you would be hurt.''

"Unless what he is working on is mishandled and we all die from it!'' she snapped.

"The substance should be relatively safe unless you sniff it, swallow some or get it on your skin. As I'm certain you know, we have serum that works against ricin, smallpox and several other dangerous agents. You would be given that beforehand, of course. Because of what he has purchased, we believe what he has is ricin or something similar.''

"You *believe?* Pardon me if I entertain some doubt. Even if the intelligence you received is credible, suppose he is attempting to alter the substance so that the immunizations will not be effective?''

Jack looked at her, sympathizing with her fears. The awful part of this was that she could easily be right.

He watched her as she sipped the remainder of her coffee, now probably tepid. But she wasn't tasting it, only going through the motions to conceal her nervous tension.

With a sigh he took the cup from her and got up to refill it. He couldn't do this after all. Too risky. She was totally unsuited for this kind of thing. And God only knew what she might suffer if Chari or his men turned out to be hostile toward women. The man was half Iranian. Too much depended solely on Chari's gratitude, his love for his son. What if he hated the kid and didn't care whether his son had a doctor's care?

Jack plunked down the cup, sloshing a few drops onto the bare table top. "I can see you aren't going to work out."

"No!" she said, shaking her head vehemently. "I will. It is simply that I had to digest all that you have told me." She managed a crooked little smile. "It does not go down well, but I see how important—no, *vital*—it is that you succeed. That *we* succeed. I must help you, of course."

He was already shaking his head. "Admirable of you to agree, but I've changed my mind, Solange."

"It is too late for that, Mercier…Jacques," she said, offering him a smile that was a bit more confident than the last. Not a full sun-on-the-water smile yet, but he saw a glimmer that could draw him in deeply enough to drown. What was it about this woman?

"You're too…honest or something. Too innocent, maybe. The boy and I will go in alone."

"I am going with you," she said decisively. Now there was fire in her eyes and a determined lift to her chin. "My father had agreed to do this and now that he cannot, I must. You need me. It is too late to alter your plan."

For the remainder of the day Solange continued to argue with Mercier when she found the chance. He shushed her whenever they were anywhere near her patient, which was most of the time.

René had roused for a while. Though he was mostly

incoherent, he did manage some of the tinned soup she had heated for their midday meal. He moved more easily now and seemed improved over the day before, despite the ordeal of being shuffled from his bed at the prison.

After he had eaten she administered more morphine. When he drifted off again, she renewed her assault on Mercier's decision to leave her somewhere and go on alone with René.

The more she considered her father's decision to assist Mercier and his people in this mission, the more determined Solange became to do so herself in his stead. Her resentment at being kept in the dark about it had faded completely. Father would have been ordered not to confide in anyone. And, of course, he would have known she would be frantic for his safety if he had told her.

She couldn't afford fear now, not for herself. There was too much at stake.

This was the first time she had really had a chance to study Mercier and take his true measure. He wore this rough exterior, his disguise, she supposed. Even that scruffy two-day beard, slightly unkempt hair and prison clothing could not conceal his real persona, not now that she knew him better.

He took total control of his surroundings. His self-confidence seemed inborn or thoroughly ingrained early in his life. There was a charisma about him that would draw people to him, make them trust him. It had worked on her to some degree even before she had known why he had abducted her and René.

There was something about this man that was unique and compelling. She suspected that it would affect almost anyone who came in contact with him. She would

need to be very careful that she did not let these bur-
geoning feelings of hers generate anything further that
could be hurtful to her. Such as an infatuation with him.
She was well aware that his qualities appealed, not just
to her but all women. And he would know this, of
course, and use it.

Her one attempt at a relationship had failed miserably
even when she'd had her emotions under strict control.
The mere thought of flinging caution to the wind with
Mercier unnerved her. If ever there would be a time for
that, it certainly was not now.

So she argued with him. Not only to set a precedent
that she would remain independent and self-sufficient,
despite his penchant for control, but because she had a
legitimate reason to disagree.

Mercier kept changing the topic of conversation, insisting on hearing all about her school days, her trials
of internship and residency and her father's work and
how she had assisted him. She shared all of the details,
hoping to convince him that she had the necessary for-
titude and experience with adversity to do what must
be done.

Later, when darkness fell, they left the cottage and
took to the road again. She would have continued trying
to change his mind, but he silenced her immediately
with a whispered warning. If René became privy to his
plans, he told her, all could be lost with regard to this
scheme.

Perhaps he believed she had given up. But Solange
had made her decision, and that was all there was to
that. They rode for what seemed hours, each lost in
thought. He was probably working out an alternate solution in his mind, one that did not require her help.

They entered a village called Tournade, according to

the road sign illuminated by the headlamps of the Saab. It was then Mercier declared his intention. ''I'm leaving you here with my people. That way you'll be nearby if the boy takes a turn for the worse.''

That said, he drove up a narrow winding street, parked on the cobblestones in front of a huge, Italianate three-story stone structure and got out. He motioned for her to do the same.

Solange did so, reluctant to leave the sleeping René. She wondered whether she would see him again if she were forced to stay in this house. It would have to be at the point of his gun. She meant to go with him.

The dark old house looked forbidding. Mercier lifted the ring on the lion's head doorknocker and rapped once, paused, then tapped four more times in rapid succession.

A tall figure opened the door and emerged immediately, a mere shadow in the weak light of the moon. The doorway and the windows of the house remained dark. Solange noted the silhouette of a weapon in the man's hand. ''You're late. We'd begun to worry,'' he said to Mercier in English. ''Everything go okay?''

''Not exactly. Will, this is Dr. Solange Micheaux, the old doctor's daughter who was filling in for him. You stay here with our passenger while I get her settled upstairs. There's no point moving young Chari any more than we need to.''

''Ma'am,'' the voice acknowledged. ''How is the boy?''

Mercier answered for her. ''Not as bad as I thought.''

''Great. Then he'll be able to vouch for you with his father.''

''I'm afraid he slept through everything,'' Mercier

said, taking Solange's arm and ushering her inside the dark building.

He led her up a winding stairway to another door and knocked again in the same sequence. A woman answered. She was armed, but when she saw Mercier, she smiled and tucked the pistol into the holster at her waist and stood aside for them to enter. The room was warmly lit, the one window completely covered with heavy black fabric that had been taped securely to the frame.

"It's about time, boss. We were getting ready to come looking for you." Her dark brown gaze landed on Solange, who had elected to remain slightly behind Mercier and as unobtrusive as possible.

"Holly Amberson, this is Dr. Solange Micheaux," he said, stepping away so the woman could see her better.

Solange admired her looks, even as she experienced a twinge of envy. Amberson was an unusual beauty with skin the color of pale caramel. Sleek black hair clipped in a short cap clung to a perfectly shaped head. Her dark brown eyes were long-lashed and slanted upward, giving her a faintly exotic expression. Her figure looked toned for strength beneath her black leggings and cropped chenille sweater. Though she stood only an inch or so taller than Solange's five-three, she exuded self-confidence.

Jacques Mercier must find this Holly person terribly attractive. Were they involved?

He spoke up then and dispelled her musings about Amberson. "The Chari boy's still in the car. Solange has him heavily sedated."

The woman nodded. "So he missed the whole rescue op he was supposed to tell his daddy about. And our option, the elder Dr. Micheaux, is in the hospital. We verified the accident last night. The driver who struck him was a plumber on his way to a job and in a hurry. He checks out clean, no ties to anyone connected with Chari. It was just an unfortunate turn of events. Tough luck, but not insurmountable. She'll do just as well.''

"No, she's staying here."

"What is my father's condition? Have you heard?" Solange demanded.

"He's doing very well. Better than expected. You need not worry about him."

"Thank you for finding out." Solange knew he would recover. She had checked his condition herself before she had gone to the prison. But it was her prerogative to worry, anyway. Their housekeeper, Marie, would be there for him if he needed anything.

Mercier interrupted her thoughts as he spoke to the woman. "I saw Will as we came in. What are the rest of the troops up to tonight?"

"Heard from Clay a couple of hours ago. He's on top of things at the office. Joe and Martine are upstairs," she added with a sly grin. "Eric's out prowling around somewhere. You want me to raise him?"

"No, that's all right. Just counting noses."

He left Solange standing there, subject to the woman's continued scrutiny and went straight to the coffee maker where he poured two cups. "I can't take Solange in with me. She's willing to help, but—"

"She knows the score?" the woman asked, eyeing Solange critically.

"Yes, everything," he admitted as he turned and handed Solange a steaming cup. He was still addressing the woman, and they were both speaking rapid English, perhaps thinking that might prevent her understanding.

"She can be trusted. That's not the problem. Still, I've elected to leave her with you."

"Why? He'll need a doctor. You were the one who said—"

"Yes, but she's not what I...*we* expected," Mercier stated flatly, as if Solange had somehow disappointed him.

Amberson gave a little mirthless laugh and shook her head. "If I thought you'd had any time to get acquainted, I'd think you'd gone sweet on her. Maybe that you didn't want to risk her cute little neck or something."

Mercier looked away while he drank his coffee, obviously not wanting to dignify that ridiculous supposition. *Sweet on her?* An idea as facetious as the expression was archaic. But it gave Solange a small lift in spirit that this gorgeous woman might think such a thing was possible. Solange, an ordinary physician, hardly felt she was exotic enough to interest a man such as Mercier. Could she have made this woman a bit jealous?

It was hard to contain her smile. She caught her bottom lip between her teeth and raised her eyebrows at the Amberson woman just because provoking her seemed the thing to do at the time.

"Good grief, man." Amberson groaned and rolled her eyes. "Tell me I'm wrong."

"You're definitely wrong," Mercier muttered. But he sounded more impatient than outraged. "We don't know much about Chari, the man. And Solange is so...well, *look* at her, Holly." He gestured in her direction rather rudely.

Solange had enough of being talked around as if she were not there at all. She interrupted in English to establish that fact. "Pardon me, but I really must insist that I accompany you, Mercier. René might—"

"She's right, Jacques," the woman said. "Who's going to tell Chari what happened? How you rescued his son?"

"I'll tell him myself."

"Yeah, right. You think he'll believe you if you just waltz in there bragging about the chances you took to get him out? That's the whole point of your going into the prison in the first place, wasn't it? To get the kid out and make the dad grateful!"

"I'll make him believe me."

Holly threw up her hands. "Jeez, then Will might as well have dragged the boy out when he was there to leave the truck! René Chari can't toot your horn for you if he's been out like a light the whole time. He won't even know who you are when he comes around."

"He saw me earlier. I interceded for him during the last beating."

Solange butted in, forming the English clearly and concisely. "But he was hurt then, probably dazed. Perhaps he won't even recognize that it was you who helped him."

Mercier growled, "I'll think of something."

Amberson threw up her hands in frustration. "Jack, be reasonable! You need her."

"You do," Solange agreed. She got right in his face to drive her point home. "If what you have told me about René's father is true, then I must do everything within my power to help prevent what he is planning. And we must find out if he is the only one doing this. This is what you told me yourself."

Amberson nodded emphatically. "She might even be able to help assess what Chari has and how much damage it might do. I've checked you out, Doc," she told Solange. "When I did the background search on your father, I did his family, too, so I'm aware of the training you've had. I wish you'd been into research in this particular area, but then, I guess you wouldn't have been where you were at the time, huh?"

Solange smiled politely. "I suppose not. However, with the sort of threats the world has been living under these past few years, I have read extensively of anthrax, smallpox, ricin and other likely weapons of terror. Most of us within the medical community realize what we might be called upon to do if such disasters occur and we have to be prepared."

"Excellent!" Amberson gave her a smile of approval that looked quite sincere. Solange returned it. She could like this woman who spoke her mind so freely and had no qualms about contradicting a man when she knew she was right.

"I *can* do this," Solange stated with conviction. "And I will."

"You see, Jack? She's actually better qualified than we'd hoped. Get her inside that lab if you can. See what he's got."

Mercier glared at his friend for a moment, then lowered his head. Obviously he was the one in charge of this assignment or whatever they were calling it, but he had to recognize that she and Amberson were right in this instance. In any event the argument seemed to be over for the moment.

Solange sat drinking her coffee while Mercier ignored them both and began typing something on one of the computers.

Holly Amberson smiled her encouragement and offered Solange a pastry from a box near the coffeemaker.

"Here, you might need some energy, however this works out."

"I *am* going," Solange said to her, then bit into the orange-glazed confection she had chosen.

"I know," Holly replied. She winked at Solange and toasted her with a croissant. "Come with me. I'll show you where to freshen up and we'll see about getting you immunized."

"That won't be necessary," Mercier said.

"Yes," Solange argued. "It will."

Chapter 3

Though he knew Holly and Solange were right, Jack hadn't conceded yet. He finished jotting down the brief report on his time at Baumettes for the record, then got up to pace out the kinks he had acquired from riding in the cramped vehicle for so many miles.

"You've had a couple of weeks to delve into Chari's history, Holly. Anything new?" he asked.

"Some," she answered, sitting down at one of the laptops and pulling up a file. "He's made three visits to his relatives in Iran. Last one was three years ago. That's confirmed. The first film he made had to do with the political unrest in the area. Went all the way back to the expulsion of the shah. Even if it had been well-done—which it wasn't—he rode the big wave too late. People everywhere were up to here with that stuff in the news."

"He got into the movie business through his wife, didn't he?" Jack said.

"Yep. She had a pretty good career going when they married, and got him on the film crew of her last picture. When it was winding down, she got pregnant. She was diabetic. After René's birth, her health went downhill fast and she died. With what she left him, Chari decided to finance his own effort. He parked the kid with her parents here in Tournade. It took him about six years to get the picture together. When it tanked, he was out of money."

"What then?"

Holly sighed. "Well, he borrowed from his in-laws, tried a couple of get-rich-quick schemes, both legit. Nothing wildly successful but he made enough to back another small production. An artsy film. Trust me, this guy has truly weird tastes in entertainment. And a humongous ego."

"That film flopped, too," Jack guessed.

"It got laughs. Most were directed at him. In the four years since, he's kept a low profile. Lived in Paris awhile. Made a couple more trips to Tehran. Soon as his in-laws died, he came back here. His son inherited the house, so Chari couldn't sell it. Can't touch René's trust fund, either."

"Unless the boy dies," Jack said, not liking that possibility at all. What if Chari had no fatherly affection at all? What if he had wanted René to stay in prison where his life would be at risk? "Did you find out if the robbery that sent the boy to Baumettes was a setup?"

"On the surface it appears he was just caught up in bad company. Maybe didn't know what was going down until he was right in the middle of it." She sighed. "No priors on him. No trouble at his schools."

"How long has Chari had all that dubious company out at the farm?"

"That's the problem. We don't know. There was that anonymous phone call to the security minister's office almost a month ago. We were brought in a few days later."

"Because he made two trips to the States last year," Jack said.

"To New York," Holly verified, "where he met with some very shady dudes our guys were keeping an eye on."

Jack nodded. He had that information already. "Okay. Fill me in on personality. I don't need the minute details you uncovered. I just need to know what he's like. What drives him."

Her lips turned up in a wry twist. "My guess would be he's sociopathic."

"Gee whiz, Holly. No wonder they pay you the big money. Seriously now."

She tapped the keyboard idly with one finger, but she wasn't even looking at the screen. No file on this, Jack realized. All of it was in Holly's head. This was where she took all facts gleaned from known actions, did her magic and constructed a profile. Her accuracy was legendary.

"He's smart and knows it, feels vastly superior to everyone else. But he lacks identity. I'm a product of two cultures myself, and Chari's two are even more diverse than mine, so I can see where he's coming from. He craves success and recognition and will do anything to get the validation he needs. I mean, *anything.*"

"But why this?" Solange asked, her voice hardly more than a whisper. "Only to finance a film? This is madness. His reasons are so…so *trivial!*"

"Not trivial to him," Holly explained. Her gaze met Jack's. "He has to have a vast amount of money and

he chose a certain way to get it. My guess is he plans
something spectacular, a big-budget thing. We're talking a *Braveheart* epic or *Dances With Wolves*. He's going for the gold and I don't mean just in his bank ac-
count. He'll want some gilded statues out of this. A
name that will go down in history like Gibson or Cost-
ner. Wouldn't surprise me much if he played a role
himself the way they did. He's got the looks. Probably
not the talent to match, but I'm sure he'll think he
does.''

"But a *movie?*" Jack asked with a huff of disbelief
that echoed Solange's. "That's just crazy."

"Well, what's he gonna do to get world recognition,
huh? He can't very well brag about snuffing a portion
of the population with poison. He's merely providing a
product that will gain him millions in ready cash to
support what he really feels compelled to do.''

Solange butted in. "Yes, but could he also desire a
bit of revenge on the public who has not accepted him
as he believes they should have done before?''

Holly nodded. "Very astute, Doctor. It could well be
that that's part of his overall plan. This guy's extremely
dangerous. He has no conscience. The laws do not apply
to him, and he feels invincible.''

"Then we'll just have to show him the light," Jack
said. He turned to Solange. "Heard enough? You see
now why I want to leave you here?''

"I'm going. We have to stop this madman."

"The plan's in place, Jack," Holly said, agreeing that
Solange was needed. "She's necessary.''

He clenched his eyes shut and shook his head. "I'm
getting really bad vibes.''

"Vibes?" Solange asked. "What does this mean?''

Jack shrugged off the question, warning Holly with

a look not to launch into any explanations right now. There wasn't time to explain fully, and even if they did, Solange could hardly be expected to give it much credit.

He had always experienced these *feelings.* That's all they were. Nothing concrete, certainly not in the category of telepathy or prescience, but they were fairly dependable. Nerves of steel and uncluttered confidence going into a mission meant success, a walk in the park. This jittery anything-that-can-go-wrong-will state of mind meant trouble. Unlike his paltry talent, Joe and Eric had the definitive visions. "What does Eric say?"

"He says he sees food. Good food. And he smells cigar smoke. This is all in the present, remember? He's tuned in on Chari."

"Joe pick up any future images at all?"

"Only one. You, all smiles. And all wet."

"Wet? What does that mean?" he asked, realizing he had repeated Solange's earlier question.

"Your hair and face are wet. And you look happy."

Solange glanced from one to the other, frowning.

Holly grinned and reached over to pinch his shoulder. "Want me to practice my Vulcan mind-meld, Captain Kirk?"

"Spare me," Jack said with a short laugh. "My mind's screwed up enough right now."

"Can't afford that," Holly said with a sigh. "I know I've been preaching concern for the individual, but now's the time to look at the overall scenario, Jack. I hate to advise it, but get back on your original track and look at the forest, will you?"

She was right, of course, but her turnaround surprised him. He tended to lump people into groups, and she had pointed that out to him. It isolated him in a way, but that was okay. It was probably what kept him sane.

Humanity, his family, his team. See them as individuals? He did in a way, but it was a very objective way. Each was part of this group or that, but if lost, the unit would survive. It could go on. *He* could go on.

He even viewed the enemy as one entity, to be erased at all costs.

With the members of his team, he considered their particular talents as they related to assignments, rated their unique performances of duty, commended or counseled them individually. That was his job. Relating to them personally, one-on-one, was a whole other thing.

He had tried that. However, after losing his favorite brother—his partner on a long ago NSA mission—and his wife in a shooting on the job two years ago, he finally had decided compartmentalizing was the only way to go. It had become habit and one that suited him. He embraced it now.

"I hear you," he said, forcing a smile. He quickly finished his coffee and set the cup down on the desk. "Well, I need to get going. Everything set up here?"

"We're good," Holly told him. "You know you can't have anything electronic on you going in."

"Yeah, they might do a sweep and find it. They'll surely check the car."

"Would they search me?" Solange offered.

"Can't risk it," Holly said. "Got your homemade shiv, Jack? They'll expect that and take it away from you, of course. Will sneaked over there earlier and left a cell phone hidden in a hollow under a stone. Look behind the second-closest tree to the house. You go out and pick it up whenever you think it's safe. You have your locator implant. We'll know exactly where you are at all times. That's something. Should we take time to insert one in the doctor?"

"No, that's not necessary. I'll signal if things go south. Or call you as soon as the threat's contained, so you can help sweep up."

"The police will come then?" Solange asked, touching his arm. Then she jerked her hand away. "They have been alerted?"

Holly frowned, looking from Solange to Jack and back again. "I thought you explained this to her."

He stood a little straighter. "It's true, there were agents out of Paris on this in the beginning, but we've requested they back off and let us handle it. As for the local police, even your intelligence warned us not to take anyone else into our confidence. Chari might have a plant somewhere inside the local force. No one knows of this but your minister of security in Paris, four of his appointed agents—two of whom are missing—and our control in the States."

"Plant?" she asked, looking confused. "Oh, someone put there to inform them. But how will you... contain the threat, as you say?"

"That's not your concern," he said abruptly. "I've got to go."

Solange watched the woman agent approach Jack and take his hands in hers. It was a gesture that spoke of a close friendship. Or perhaps something more intimate. "You be careful out there, you hear me? You promised me a week in Paris and I have it in writing."

"Like you'd let me forget it," he said, giving the Amberson woman a tight but reassuring smile. "See you soon, Holly."

"Yeah, see ya," she repeated in a fierce whisper.

Solange followed Mercier down the stairs and slipped out the front door behind him.

The man called Will shook his hand. "Be seeing you, Jack."

"Sure, take it easy," Mercier answered.

Solange hurried around to the passenger side and got in, fastening her seat belt even before Jack settled behind the wheel.

It must be a tradition among the members of his small cadre not to say goodbye, Solange thought to herself. But she could hardly help wishing someone had at least wished them farewell.

She took a deep breath and looked in back at the sleeping René. She could only hope his father was glad to see him and his rescuers. Glad enough not to question whether they might have concealed their real reasons for imposing upon his hospitality.

Jack could do nothing but think about what he could be exposing this young woman to. He needed someone older, tougher. At the edge of the village, they passed a train station, dark now, deserted. He suddenly pulled over and stopped the car near a phone booth. "Do you have any euros?"

"Some. In my bag. You need them?"

He reached between the seats and retrieved her medical bag, then set in on her knees. "No, but you will. Don't argue with me, Solange. Take this and get out of the car. I'm going to call Will to come and get you and take you home. But first I want your word that you won't reveal any of what we've shared with you to anyone. I've told you about the possibility of informants among the police. Lives are at risk and you have made an oath to save lives. Do I have your promise?"

She looked deeply into his eyes for a long time, then cast a glance into the back seat to make certain René was not awake. "No. For the last time, I will not let you go without me."

Jack shook his head, willing her to understand. "He's only one boy, Solange. Think of the people who will not receive your help in the future if you don't survive this."

"But I thought you agreed back there that I could come. I trust you to protect me."

Jack peered out the window into the darkness. "I would die trying, but there are no guarantees that would help. I don't want to risk you. Get out."

"Do this and I will go straight to the police. There might be one among them who works for Chari, but if they all know what is happening and go in immediately, they will arrest everyone and this will be over."

Oh, great. "That can't happen, Solange. I need to be there for a while first, to see whether he's already deployed any of the substance. There could be a shootout if the police burst in. If everyone there dies, we'd never know if the stuff is already out there until some terrorist uses it. Or Chari could be notified before the police arrive, move his operation where we couldn't locate him. Will you give me your word you won't alert anyone?"

"No," she replied without hesitation. "You will have to take me with you." She set the bag on the floorboard. "This is also my fight. My people are at risk if this man tests this here. And even if he does not do so, there will be others to die elsewhere if he succeeds in selling it. You must stop him, and I must help you do it. Let us go now." She sat back, her arms folded across her chest.

He surrendered. If he left her, she would probably follow, alone or with the local police. Either could be catastrophic. "I want you to vow on whatever you hold sacred that you'll do exactly what I tell you. Nothing more, nothing less."

To her credit, she thought about it before answering. "I will do as you say."

Jack cranked the car and rolled on, leaving the village of Tournade behind. "Be sure, Doctor, because we have less than fifteen kilometers to go. Then you'll be committed for good."

"You must trust me."

"After you have just blackmailed me the way you did?"

"Even so," she replied.

Solange worried more about Mercier's survival than about René's. There was no way for her to know how well equipped he was to handle this intrigue. He must be good at what he did or his government would never have sent him to do this. At least they had chosen one proficient in the language. And as stubborn as any man she'd ever met. She couldn't deny he knew how to fight. The guard he had overpowered could attest to that.

This man needed her. He had admitted as much. Why had he changed his mind about that? she wondered. Had she seemed too weak and helpless to be of any use? That made her all the more determined to prove him wrong.

She felt terrible that René must soon undergo a shock when he learned about his father's treachery. Who was to say what sort of father Chari was? If what he had chosen to become involved with was any indication, he could not possess a shred of compassion.

The boy was barely seventeen. He had passed his recent birthday locked away. Had any visitor come to see him? She doubted it, because those with someone on the outside who furnished the inmates with money and things to trade usually fared better than René had done.

France's prisons were a disgrace. Her brother had died in LaTerre, innocent of embezzlement and awaiting the trial that had never come to pass. Solange's father had worked hard since then, trying to ameliorate some of the damage done in those hellholes. Solange was helping to carry on that mission.

There were times when they had no patients at Baumettes. Guards would lock everyone down and refuse them treatment. Some days after bandaging knife wounds, treating drug overdoses and the various illnesses caused by overcrowding, malnutrition and nonexistent hygiene, both she and her father despaired of making any difference at all.

Then they had come upon René, a boy so like Gerard had been. Young, weak of body, beautiful in appearance and fair game for the bullies of the world. Perhaps he was not innocent of the robbery they said he committed—she might never know the truth of that—but she did know that he did not deserve to be beaten half to death. She wanted to get him released, make him well again and help him get on with his life. To save one. Just one would make it all worth doing.

Now perhaps she could save not only René, but other people who had no clue yet that they were even in peril. Solange had never seen firsthand results of biological warfare, but she could well imagine how dire they would be. There would be little or maybe nothing she could do after the fact if it occurred, so she simply must prevent it by whatever means she could.

They turned onto a road leading through a stand of

poplars and wound their way for several miles to a huge, rambling old manor house. The farmland around it lay fallow for the most part. Someone had planted what appeared to be oats in one of the fields adjacent to the main road.

"Well, here we are," Mercier said as they stopped at the front entrance. Two dark-skinned men approached, armed with automatic weapons and menacing looks. The larger of the two ordered them out of the car.

Solange obeyed immediately. Jack did so a bit more languidly, gesturing as he explained in perfect colloquial French that they had brought Mr. Chari's son to him, along with the doctor who had saved his life. He told them that the boy was unconscious and needed a litter.

Solange had thought it best that René not be conscious when they arrived. As in the prison, the worse his health seemed, the better it would be for him. At least for now.

One of the men disappeared inside and returned shortly with a distinguished-looking man of around forty. He was dark-haired, black-eyed and his skin color—as did his given name—suggested Mediterranean blood. He was slight of build, though possessing a sort of wiry strength his son had not yet acquired. Solange knew simply by the resemblance in their features that this had to be Ahmed Chari.

The guard with him aimed his weapon directly at Solange's head as Chari approached the car's back door and opened it. His sharp, assessing gaze traveled over his son. Then he asked her, "What has happened to him?"

"He was beaten by the guards at Baumettes Prison.

For insolence, so they said when I arrived to treat him. They realized he was of some importance when advised of his identity, and so they brought him to the infirmary to be treated.'' Solange knew the majority of the prisoners in French jails were Islamic. The places were terrorist breeding grounds these days. Perhaps Chari had some influence in those circles. His current activities certainly made that probable. Why had he not used it?

''Will he recover?'' Chari asked, hiding his concern as a father rather well, if indeed he had any. Though he was quite handsome, she had never seen a colder countenance on anyone. Merely looking at him gave her a chill.

''Yes, I believe he will eventually,'' she answered truthfully, ''but he has had some internal damage. Surgery was not indicated at the time, but it might well become necessary later if he has continued problems.''

''You have been treating him from the first?''

''He suffered alone those first two days before they brought him to the infirmary.''

Chari turned to the guards. ''Carry the boy inside. Put him in his old room, the nursery on the first floor, and bring in a cot for the doctor.'' Then he looked at Mercier. ''Get rid of him.''

''Wait!'' Solange cried. ''He saved René's life! It was he who overpowered the guard responsible for your son's beating! Is this how you reward his good deed?''

Chari looked at her as if really seeing her for the first time. She almost shivered under his regard. ''What is this man to you?'' he demanded.

''Nothing at all,'' Solange declared. ''But he did save your son's life and I simply do not believe you should kill a man for doing you so great a favor!''

''Kill him, Doctor? I merely wanted him sent away.''

Slowly Chari shifted his attention back to the object of their conversation. "So who are you and what offense sent you to the prison?"

"Jacques Mercier. They say I was involved in receiving stolen weapons, but…" he let his voice taper off with a shrug of his shoulders.

"Get on the radio, Piers, and contact Vaughn in Marseilles. See if this man is lying. If he is not, bring him to my study."

With that, Chari walked back into the house and disappeared. Solange's frantic gaze connected with Mercier's. Neither spoke, but the look he gave her betrayed a brief hint of gratitude and even a little surprise. Her own expression must have been wild-eyed with fright, though she was trying hard not to show how terrified she felt.

Two more men came out carrying a frayed and faded litter that might have been scavenged during World War II. Gently, at her direction, they transferred René from the back seat of the car onto the carrier.

She reluctantly abandoned Mercier to his fate as she accompanied her patient into his father's house. One of the guards gave a cursory check for weapons hidden beneath her clothing and then plundered more carefully through her medical bag. Satisfied, they left her alone with René. She tried not to let herself wonder whether she would ever be allowed outside the house again in her lifetime. Or if Jack Mercier would ever see the inside of it during his.

Later, after suffering a humiliating and thorough body search and waiting for Piers to make his phone call to Marseilles, Jack relaxed a little. He was inside. Next step accomplished.

He attempted to put all thoughts of Solange Micheaux out of his mind when he arrived in Chari's study. She was in even more danger than he had worried she would be. He had figured Chari would be a little more grateful for his son's survival and that he would treat Solange with some respect because of her part in that. Apparently, the man had little in the way of paternal feelings and no kind regard at all for females.

Jack now wished he had opened that car door in Tournade, shoved her out forcefully, then sped off before she knew what had happened. Right now she'd be under no threat whatsoever if he'd done that.

But then again, he could be dead now if she had not come along. If she hadn't interceded with Chari, he'd probably be out in one of those fields with a little dirt kicked over him.

"Sit down, Mercier," Chari instructed. "Cigar?"

Jack reached forward and took one. He hated the stinking things, but some men thought smoking them together was a bonding experience. If Chari were one of those men, Jack certainly did want to accommodate him. A little bonding was needed right about now.

"Drink?" Chari offered, gesturing lazily with one hand at the sideboard.

Two fancy decanters stood there wearing a coat of dust. Did Chari practice the religion that forbade it or was he just careful not to let alcohol fuzz up his brain? In either case, Jack wasn't about to break any unspoken rules.

"No, thanks. Never touch it."

Chari smiled his approval. "Good. We should get down to business. Tell me about these weapons you have allegedly imported."

Jack shrugged and took a puff of the cigar before he

answered. "A man called Jurin hired me to pick up a delivery in Narbonne. I drove there, went where he directed me to go. The police were waiting. They hauled me in along with the men who had actually had possession of the shipment when they arrived. I was in Baumettes awaiting trial. You know how that goes."

"Unfortunately." Chari picked a speck of tobacco off his lip with his fingernail. "How did you come to rescue René?"

"I saw the guards knocking him around. He looked like a kid who didn't need to be where he was. When I got a look at his doctor, I figured she didn't need to be there, either. So…since I had no love at all for the bastard who used his fists on children, I took him out. Then I took them with me." He smiled. "I was going anyway, you see."

"You had to have help. Baumettes is fairly secure, but even I could not find a way to liberate René."

Jack somehow doubted he had tried all that hard. Will Griffin had encountered no problem in bribing the right people. Be that as it may, Chari was the one Jack had to deal with right now. And he had to convince Chari he would be a valuable asset.

"You're right. I did have someone on the outside. He crossed a few palms, got the right key, the right vehicles."

"Where is he now?"

Jack smiled. "I had no further use for him."

"How did you find your way here?" Chari asked. "The work I am doing requires solitude. I have made certain that few people know my address."

"René mentioned the location when he was delirious with fever," Jack lied. "I hoped that out of gratitude you might offer me a position here."

"And how would you know what sort of business I am in and what work might be available?"

Jack sighed and rolled the cigar between his fingers. He met Chari's gaze directly and smiled. "I understand you make films. I confess I have not seen any of them, but I am not much acquainted with the arts."

"The last was well received in Cannes four years ago," Chari informed him with a haughty sniff.

Jack almost laughed. The film had tanked miserably and the public screening had proved a joke. Chari had delusions of grandeur that made Napoleon seem modest.

"I've heard that you live a reclusive life. Whatever it is you are doing now, I can ensure that you remain undisturbed."

Chari nodded. "Do you trust this helper you hired for the escape not to have followed you here?" Chari watched him carefully, his eyes narrowed. "I do not wish more unexpected company."

"You are not making a film," Jack observed.

"No. Where is the man who helped you?"

"I do not believe in loose ends," Jack said. The pinball dropped in place. Jack could almost hear the *kaching* declaring him a winner with the only correct answer.

"Perhaps I could use a man of your...experience," Chari said, though he still wore the suspicious look Jack figured he'd been born with.

"You need not worry that the police will come here seeking the boy. As far as the authorities know, we are headed out of the country. We will have been observed and reported."

"By someone else who could change a story and be-

tray you. I believe you have too many accomplices,''
Chari declared.

"No, this was just an acquaintance who owed me a
favor. She made a phone call for the false report, but
has no idea where I am at present." Jack smiled. "I try
to plan for all contingencies."

"You are hired."

"Thank you. How is the pay?"

"Excellent once the job is complete. You won't need
it before then." Chari stood, a sign that the conversation
was finished as far as he was concerned.

Jack had a sneaky feeling Chari never intended to
issue any paychecks when his project was over. In view
of that, he thought he might as well risk making a better
deal with the new boss. Maybe come to an arrangement
that might offer Solange more safety.

"One more thing," Jack said boldly.

"Yes?"

"I'll settle for half pay, get rid of any…loose ends
you have dangling when you've done whatever it is
you're up to. Also I will make certain you're not followed if you decide to change locations."

"And what would secure your generosity in this regard?" Chari asked slyly. "A little medical attention,
perhaps?"

Jack grinned and stubbed out his cigar in the lead
crystal ashtray on Chari's desk. "Precisely. Have we an
agreement?"

"Sounds reasonable. You calm her fears, see that she
takes care of the boy and make her enjoy her stay well
enough that she won't make any attempt to leave or
contact anyone. If she does, you are to prevent it and
then dispose of her immediately. Can you do that, Mercier?"

"Of course. I assume you are not interested in her yourself, then?" He needed to make certain of that. If Chari made any move on Solange, Jack knew he would have to kill him, even if it blew the mission. He would just have to perform whatever damage control he could after that.

Chari frowned. "She is beautiful, but I dislike women who believe themselves intelligent. I detest the ones who really *are*."

Jack laughed as if it were a joke, but he knew better. Chari was speaking with conviction at this point. "She's smart all right."

"Has she any experience in a laboratory?" Chari asked, idly tapping the ash off his cigar, fastidiously extending his smallest finger.

Jack shrugged, not really wanting to seem too curious. "I could ask her. We aren't all that well acquainted. Yet," he added meaningfully.

"Do so. She might be able to assist with what I have initiated if you could persuade her to cooperate. Find out what you can about her experience and report to me in the morning. Meanwhile, make yourself useful. See Piers for your accommodation and the schedule for the day."

Jack nodded. "He is your second in command, is he not?"

"Very observant, Mercier. Tell him to give you the old au pair's room that is adjacent to my son's. The woman may visit you, but she is to sleep on her cot in the room with René."

Jack sauntered out. He wanted to run directly to Solange and see that she was all right, but he knew better. Instead, he searched out Piers, the only one of Chari's goons who appeared to have any brains to go with his brawn.

He found him in the kitchen stirring a huge pot of soup. "Smells wonderful," Jack said. "Since we got so intimately acquainted with that body search, I hope I can charm you out of a bowl of that later on."

Piers grunted. It could have been a chuckle. Jack leaned over the stove and inhaled deeply, his eyes closed. "Tarragon, eh? Confess, you were once a chef."

"If I may offer you a bit of free advice, Mercier? Speaking the first thought that enters your head can be lethal in this place."

Piers sounded less provincial than the other men Jack had encountered here. Like Chari, he seemed much better educated than the rest.

The calluses on the outer edges of his hands betrayed training in martial arts. Those on the tips of the fingers of his left hand indicated he was probably a guitarist. The spices he used in the soup—several more than the tarragon Jack had mentioned—revealed the man had more than a rudimentary interest in cuisine. A real Renaissance man, this one.

He looked to be somewhere between thirty-five and forty, and dressed much the same as the other guards in jeans and long-sleeved pullovers, topped with a pocketed vest. Clips for his weapons were just visible, peeking above the edge of the pockets like naughty gremlins.

Jack wondered where to obtain the uniform of the well-dressed terrorist around here. He felt out of place in his grim blue prison uniform, but didn't imagine he would be allowed to go shopping right away. The thought of asking made him smirk a little.

Piers frowned at that, probably wondering what he was up to. Jack decided he'd better alleviate that curiosity. "Mr. Chari said you should give me orders as to my activities and then direct me to the room next to René's where I'll be staying."

"Fine. Dinner is at eight."

"Evening attire?" Jack quipped.

Piers chuckled.

"Seriously, I could use some other clothes if there are any available." Jack plucked at his collar and grimaced.

Piers continued stirring his soup. "On the way to your room, we will stop by mine. We are the same size."

So they were. That was good for the clothes issue. Not good if they ever squared off hand to hand, which they might in the near future if Jack could not secure a weapon before the big showdown.

"You will take the evening watch on the roof from nine to midnight," Piers told him. "If you sight anything moving, you are to alert the others. When it is time, I will furnish you a handset, programmed to the correct frequency, and night vision goggles."

He put down his long-handled spoon, carefully resting the bowl of it on a saucer, then wiped his hands on a dish towel. "Come with me."

Jack felt the punch of relief that always came with a successful infiltration. Chari suspected nothing and would accept him as one of the hirelings. No problem there.

The only thing that worried Jack now was ensuring that Solange had a purpose as far as Chari was concerned.

Once René was well, unless she had another task to complete for him, their host might see her as excess baggage.

In one way it was fortunate that Chari had suggested she work in the laboratory. At least Jack hadn't had to suggest it himself. On the other hand, Jack could hardly stand to think of allowing her into the potentially dangerous facility.

He had never wrestled with this kind of apprehension when Holly embarked on a dangerous aspect of a mission. Even when Maribeth had gone undercover on the job, he hadn't been this on edge.

They had been well-trained operatives, of course. Maybe that was why. They were as prepared as they could be.

But his gut told him that was not it. Solange had touched something inside him no one else had ever reached.

Chapter 4

Solange heard voices in the next room. She pressed her ear against the door and listened, recognizing one of the men as Mercier. A huge wave of relief washed over her. She had begun to fear that her intervention on his behalf had proved unsuccessful after all.

She waited for at least a quarter hour after she heard the other man leave and close the door. Figuring he'd had plenty of time to go elsewhere in the house and not overhear her talking to Mercier, she then opened the door and quietly slipped inside the room.

"Solange?" Mercier exclaimed as he exited the door facing the one she had entered. His hair was wet, his week's worth of beard shaved. And he stood there naked as the day he was born.

She blinked hard, but found she was unable to keep her eyes shut. Solange had seen more than her share of male bodies in her time, but this one blew her doctor's detachment away completely. Perhaps it was the way he moved, his well-honed muscles flexing with a silent strength and grace that piqued both admiration and fascination. His was not a physique built for show, but for action. For *use*. The very thought made her shiver with anticipation.

"I...I suppose I should have knocked."

"That's all right," he said, sounding unaffected by the intrusion, "since we're destined to be lovers. You might as well see what you're up against."

Lovers? Shock would have kept her silent even if he hadn't raised a finger to his lips in warning. He walked toward her, wrapping a towel around his waist as he moved.

Solange came to her senses and backed up a step just as he reached her.

He beckoned her closer, then placed one hand on her shoulder and leaned forward to whisper in her ear. "They are listening. Follow my lead." Then he stood away and said in a normal voice, "Don't look so surprised, Doctor. A woman such as you cannot go unclaimed for long in a houseful of men. If you remain unattached, it could cause trouble in the ranks."

She cleared her throat, trying to focus on anything other than him. The room in which they stood provided little in the way of distractions. The plaster was cracked, the paint peeling in places. The furniture consisted of a table, a chair and a large double bed.

She forced her gaze back to Mercier rather than look at that item. "I am here only to improve René's health. Suppose I do not wish to become...involved with you?"

He smiled. It totally changed his countenance and Solange couldn't tear her gaze away. "Ah, but you *do* wish it," he said in a seductive growl. "A man knows

these things. You want me. I can see it in those gorgeous blue eyes.''

Eyes which she now rolled at such blatant boasting.
Could he see it? Was he serious?

He pulled a comical face and pinched her shoulder
gently to show that he was merely acting. ''Come now,
Solange. Be reasonable. Kiss me as you did last night,
hmm? You were not so haughty then, eh?''

Her mouth dropped open with a disbelieving scoff
that he would go so far with this charade. Was this
really necessary?

He grinned. After a moment of pregnant silence, he
sighed loudly and spoke again. ''Enough for now. We
had best not get too carried away and forget why you're
here. You should see to the boy.''

But instead of allowing her to do that, he took her
by the arm and quickly drew her into the lavatory.
There, he turned on the water faucet. ''To cover the
sound of our words,'' he explained in a hurried whisper.
''Chari has both bedrooms bugged, voice activated
transmitters. We'll leave the devices operational most
of the time so he won't suspect we know. You'll have
to play along. Can you handle it?''

She puffed out her cheeks and expelled a breath, then
met his worried gaze. ''It seems I have no choice.''

He smiled again and touched her face. Just one finger
along her cheek. ''It will be all right, Solange. Please
don't be afraid. Not of me, anyway.''

She looked around the small enclosure, which was
still steamy from his bath. ''I hope there aren't any cameras. You did say he was into films.''

''I thought of that first thing and checked it out. With
the heavy plaster, it would be too difficult to conceal

them in the walls or ceiling. However, the exits and corridors are covered, I noticed."

"He will kill me when I'm no longer needed. I saw it in his eyes," she said with conviction. "As soon as he thinks René is well enough to do without me."

To Mercier's credit, he didn't bother with false reassurances. Instead he asked, "How soon will that be?"

"I've told you, he is not as severely hurt as I pretended. I have kept administering more morphine than needed so that we would not have to explain things to him. When I discontinue that medication, he should be conscious within a few hours and perfectly well within a week."

"How are your supplies?"

"Almost exhausted," she admitted. "Only two more doses. My father or I only visited the prison once a day and administered enough to keep him sedated until one of us could return. It is too dangerous to carry around a large supply of a controlled substance, especially in that environment."

"I see your point. The boy might as well be allowed to come around soon, anyway. Chari might order you to help out in the lab."

"Isn't that what you were hoping he would do?"

He shook his head and ran a hand over his face. "I don't know, Solange. It's so risky."

"This entire errand is a risk, Jacques. I only hope I can manage to do all that is necessary," she whispered.

She felt his strong hand clasp her upper arm. "It could be deadly if you don't know what you're doing, Solange. Tell me now if you aren't sure, and I'll do my level best to get you out of here."

He would try to get her safely away. But she knew

that the chance of his succeeding was very poor, given present circumstances.

"I have to go in if he will allow it. You need to know what they have made in the lab and what they might have done with it so far."

He nodded. "Or what they plan to do. But if you agree to do this, you have to pretend to help them. You might be involved in the actual production of this stuff. You do know the proper precautions to take when handling substances like ricin?"

His hand on her arm had increased the intensity of its grip. Solange realized he was afraid for her. Really afraid, to the point where he might risk this vital mission if she seemed reluctant.

"I know what to do," she assured him, putting more conviction into her answer than she truly felt. "Perhaps I can be of more help than you think."

In a surprising move, he put his arms around her and held her close. "I wish to God I had left you where you were. You're not cut out for this."

She pushed against his chest until she could look him straight in the eye. "Do not underestimate me, Mercier. While it is true I have not been trained at deception, I now have enormous incentive to learn very quickly. Modesty aside, when I decide to do a thing, I excel at it. That is how, against extremely heavy odds, I became a physician."

He smiled down at her, a kind smile, still holding her in his arms. "My mistake." Their eyes met and held. Then he lowered his mouth to hers and kissed her.

Solange felt the firmness of his lips soften against hers. She waited for him to begin grasping and probing, injecting passion and heat into the caress, but he did none of that. His kiss remained just that, a caress. Still, she felt it to her soul. It seemed to thaw something frozen inside her.

How long had it been since someone had cared about her welfare, worried for her safety, offered to defy death in order to remove her from danger? Certainly not since she was nine years old and lost her beloved mother. Even then, her father had not gone out of his way to caution her about anything, to smooth the way for her in life. He had only taken a real interest in her after she had struggled through medical school and residency and become one of his peers.

Her one lover when she was a resident at St. Evelyn's had been little more than a roommate who alternated duties with her in the emergency room. Jean had never kissed her in the soulful way Jacques had just done. He had never made her feel this way. They had parted after eight months, almost with relief, when he had secured a position in Strasbourg.

His coldness must have affected her more than she had realized. Since Jean, she had shied away from establishing an intimate relationship with anyone and directed all of her energy into her work. Until now she had been quite content with that. She had believed it was *she* who lacked passion. Well, she certainly knew better now.

However, Jacques Mercier was not a man to build fantasies around. He was a spy. He lived his life as other people. He told lies for a living. She had witnessed how brutally he could behave. And yet he could also be infinitely gentle and caring.

Prudence and caution demanded she question that behavior. It could be but another pretense of his. Something he used to control her.

She pushed completely away from him and pulled

her mantle of professionalism about her like a protective cloak. "I need no persuasion to do what needs doing, Jacques. You may relax."

He laughed a little, the sound wry. "That's what you think? That this is meant as persuasion? If I believed kissing you would work, I would have kissed you good-bye in Tournade."

Then he turned her around and patted her playfully on the bottom. "Go, Solange. See about your patient."

She went, but not before she caught a quick glimpse of the effect their kiss had on his body. He was definitely not relaxed. And something in her other than that frozen section of her soul had responded just as readily to him.

Perhaps they would become lovers. If she survived this, he might make a wonderful memory for her. And if she did not survive it, this would be her last chance to experience anything resembling intimacy.

She had seen firsthand how well Jacques could pretend. She could do that, too. If nothing else, she was a quick study.

The next day passed uneventfully. At dinner Jack remembered what Holly had said about Eric's psychic observation. He'd been right. The cuisine proved excellent, though the company certainly did lack charm.

To Jack's immense relief, Solange either had elected to eat alone in her room or had been ordered to do so. If Chari was deliberately keeping her away from his men, that could only be a good thing.

After dinner Piers directed Jack to his lookout post and left him there. He was not allowed a weapon, of course. Several other guards, armed, were scattered equidistant around the rooftops. Now and then there would be the flick of a lighter and then the glow of a cigarette, these and the dark, shifting silhouettes of the men with automatic rifles were the only movements Jack saw while on the roof.

The moon cast its weak glow over the landscape. It was easy enough to spot the trees. He located the second-nearest one, which he knew concealed the cell phone and other accouterments the Sextant team had left there for him. No way he could retrieve those without being observed, but other than reassuring the team he was still alive, he had no need for them yet, anyway.

The night remained quiet, no sign of anyone or anything attempting to approach the grounds. The main road lay too far off to hear traffic if there was any.

How serene it seemed out here in the countryside. How deceptively benign this quiet peace, when in reality there were weapons of death and destruction filling the house beneath him.

Jack reflected on death—not the natural passing that old age or illness produced, but the killings. He thought how he had seen too much of it in his thirty-five years. Strangers, friends, his brother and his beloved wife, all victims of brutal, senseless acts of terror. He, too, would probably become another of the early-death statistics one of these days, but not before he rid the world of at least one more monster who had no regard for life. Ahmed Chari.

When his watch was over, one of the other men relieved Jack, handing him a flashlight to find his way back downstairs.

The urge to go exploring and try to find the lab almost overcame him, but he knew now was not the time. Unless Chari was a complete idiot, Jack knew his host would have someone watching the new guy very closely.

He passed through the room where Solange lay sleeping on the cot placed near the boy's bed. Though he wanted to stop, he did not. She needed all the rest she could get. Her mind must be absolutely clear and focused when she entered that lab, if in fact Chari decided to put her to work there. Jack got a cold chill just thinking about it, but she was his best hope of getting the pertinent information needed before destroying this setup.

He went straight to bed and fell into a light sleep, an old and useful trick he had learned long ago in the Army's Special Ops where insomnia could be a dangerous enemy. So could sleeping too deeply.

The sound of voices from the next room woke him. Faint light spilled around the door that he had left half open. He pulled on the heavy twill pants Piers had given him earlier and crept close to listen.

Solange spoke soothingly. "It is coming off the morphine that makes you feel this way, René. I cannot give you more."

"Poison!" the boy rasped. "I do not wish you to give me more. I *hate* drugs. I told you and the old doctor from the beginning, I would rather have the pain."

"As soon as you have eaten something, you will feel better. No, do not try to rise yet!" her voice grew louder, more commanding.

"But I must! I cannot stay here in this place," he complained.

"Nonsense, this is your home, René," she argued.

He scoffed at that. "You understand nothing, doctor. My father will not be happy I have returned."

"All fathers and sons are at odds now and then. It's

perfectly natural to disagree. But you know he loves you and wants you to be well again."

"He hates me. I remind him of my mother. But he is wrong there. I am not weak."

"There, there. Be calm. Try to sleep again and we will discuss all of this later."

Jack entered the room. Solange turned, frowning at him. She wore a faded red T-shirt bearing the flaking image of a black motorcycle on the front, obviously an old one of René's. Her legs and feet were bare. With her hair tousled around her face and her eyes that wide and frightened, she appeared even younger than her patient.

"Who are you?" René demanded. He sat up, slid off the bed and shook his fist at Jack. "One of my father's men? If you bother my doctor, I will kill you!"

The anger and fear in René's eyes was more than adolescent rebellion. The boy knew, or at least suspected, that there was real danger here, for himself and for the woman who had saved him.

Jack made a sudden decision. If René knew what his father was involved in and started slinging accusations around right now, they were all as good as dead. Probably the boy, too.

If Chari knew René was already aware of his plans, it wouldn't take a genius to figure out why Jack had shown up here with him.

He raised a finger to his lips, hurried over to the nightstand beside the bed and pointed to the underside, then tapped on his ear with his finger.

An owl-eyed René opened his mouth to speak, but Solange quickly pressed her hand over it. "René, dear, this is Jacques Mercier. It was he who brought you out of Baumettes and home to your father."

René was busy bending over to look beneath the table at the tiny instrument Jack had pointed out. He nodded slowly as he straightened, holding his injured ribs with one hand.

Solange tried to help him back into bed, but he waved her off and climbed in by himself. "I suppose I must thank you for your trouble, sir. But why in heaven's name did you have to bring *her* along?"

"What's the problem? Don't you like her?" Jack asked, allowing a note of sarcasm.

"Of course I *like* her! But she shouldn't..." He glanced again at the table and back at Jack. "Escapes are dangerous. She could have been hurt."

"To tell you the truth, she got in the way. Wouldn't allow me to take you unless she came, too."

"Wait! I remember you now. I saw you the day...you stopped them beating me, didn't you?"

"Try not to read too much into that. It was my chance to relieve Bernier of that handmade knife he was so damned proud of."

René lay back on the pillows and closed his eyes. "Again, thank you. But I wish you had left me on my own once you got me out of there." It was clear he devoutly wished that.

With a sudden note of hope, he added, "Do you think my father would allow you both to accompany me out of the country? We could go to Spain!"

Jack looked at Solange as she sighed. Then he shook his head. "No, René, I think not. You will be safer here than traveling around. The police will be searching for all three of us."

The boy's face twisted with disgust as he opened his eyes and met Jack's gaze directly. He looked sick at heart. A wealth of understanding passed between them.

Jack could see that René knew precisely what sort of threat they faced. He knew what was going on.

René nodded, his expression a curious mixture of apology, disgust and fright. Jack didn't need telepathy to realize that René was the one who had contacted the authorities about the lab.

The boy was also was quick enough to put together exactly why Jack had really come here.

Does your father know it was you who made the call? Jack mouthed the words and pantomimed, making no sound whatsoever.

René slowly shook his head and his lips formed the word *no*. Then he offered a slender hand to Jack and they shook firmly, as men do when united in a cause.

Obviously, the son possessed a humanity lacking in the father, thank God. It was possible, even probable, that Chari had René framed in order to keep him in prison and out of the way. Jack wondered how this might impact the mission.

"Go back to sleep," Jack advised, speaking normally. "Until the doctor and your father decide you're able to travel, you won't be going anywhere. At any rate, it will be some time yet before you can even walk."

René gave a thumbs-up signal to show he understood he was to remain bedridden. He smiled at Solange, then at Jack and sighed audibly, as if relieved to have someone in his corner at last. With a final nod, he closed his eyes.

The boy wasn't well by any means. He was coming down off morphine, muscles weak from inactivity and had to be hurting like hell with those bruised ribs. The brief and sudden spate of activity had exhausted him. But the young bounce back like rubber balls.

René's youthful enthusiasm might too easily work to their disadvantage once he had recuperated a little more and grew bored with inactivity. It was anyone's guess how this new ally of theirs would respond to instructions.

Jack wished for their sakes, as well as René's, that the little doctor had brought enough drugs to last these next few days.

Solange brushed the tousled hair off René's sweaty forehead, a motherly gesture that seemed very natural for her, then got up and headed for her rumpled cot. She moved slowly as if she were very tired.

"Good night, Jacques," she said.

"Not yet, but it could be," he replied, knowing the bug would pick up their words. "Come with me."

She glanced again at René who appeared to be sleeping, then back at Jack. "I should stay in here."

"We'll hear him if he wakes up again. Come in for an hour."

"A whole *hour?*" She put a smirk in her voice that made Jack smile.

"More if you like. I can be very inventive."

"Let me brush my teeth first. I still taste all of that garlic from the stew."

"I'll be waiting," Jack said in what he hoped was a seductive voice.

He hurried her into the bathroom, switched on the light and then turned on the water so they couldn't be overheard. "Well, this is it, Solange. You're sure you want to go through with it?"

She nodded. "We have to. What shall I do?"

"Act naturally. Don't ham it up too much." He grinned. "Unless you feel moved to it."

"What…what are you going to do?"

"Nothing you won't love. Relax." He turned off the water tap, took her by the hand and led her to his bed. He had left on the light in the bathroom so she could see how to get back to her own bed later. And so he could see her.

The springs creaked when he sat down. "Now let's remove this," he said with a sly chuckle. He tugged the hem of the borrowed shirt but didn't offer to lift it. "Ah, what have you been hiding from me, *ma chére*? Look at you! Here, lie down." With an encouraging pat on her shoulder, he pushed her facedown on the bed. She looked over her shoulder, frowning up at him in the lamp light.

"Relax and enjoy it," he crooned. "You are entirely too tense, love." He slid his warm palms up her back and gently grasped her shoulders, massaging her shoulder blades with his thumbs.

She sighed audibly and then groaned. "Um, that feels...so good."

"Yes," he said, sounding breathless. "This? You like?"

He changed the position of his hands and worked the muscles along her spine. The soft sounds she made had him sweating. They were entirely too close to what they were pretending to be. His body reacted predictably enough.

He shifted on the bed, putting a knee on either side of her hips, causing the vintage bed to squeak appropriately each time he moved. When he could stand no more, Jack pinched her playfully, along her rib cage. She cried out at the surprise move and struggled wildly against the tickling.

As climaxes went, it left a lot to be desired, but the sound effects were fairly convincing.

Jack released and moved off of her, collapsing on his back with a true groan of relief. "Enough?"

She giggled. Actually giggled. Jack silenced her with a kiss. He just couldn't help himself. He had been wanting to do that again, and now seemed the time.

He forced himself to come up for air, realizing if he didn't, this could become the real deal, whether she wanted it to or not. And she just might, he admitted, given the way she kissed him back.

"You are a very unusual man, Jacques Mercier," she whispered. He doubted the mike in the lamp table picked that up. He wasn't even certain if she meant it to.

"Thanks," he gasped. "I've never met a woman quite like you, either."

She rolled off the bed and pulled the hem of shirt down to cover her panties. "May I come again?"

"All right, but I'll need a few minutes." He laughed and crossed his arms behind his head, loving the way she blushed when he teased her.

"Tomorrow night," she said, her voice pure silk. "Then it will be your turn." She injected so much promise in that drawn-out suggestion, he almost took her at her word.

"Good night, Jacques."

"Absolutely. You have an indisputable talent for this, Solange."

"I know," she agreed. "Sometimes I even surprise myself."

He watched the provocative sway of her hips as she disappeared into the bathroom. The water came on, the old pipes clunking within the walls. A few moments later she opened the door, switched off the light and disappeared into the other room to finish what was left of the night on the narrow cot close to her patient.

Jack tried to go back to sleep, but none of the relaxation tricks he'd been taught had prepared him for shutting off what Solange stirred up inside him. The arousal would ebb eventually, but there was something deeper that wouldn't subside.

He lay awake until dawn, still feeling the sweet play of her muscles beneath his hands, reliving her sighs of pleasure, inhaling the scent she had left behind. And worrying what tomorrow might bring for her.

Chapter 5

The next night Solange went to Jack's bed again. His smile reassured her as he took her hand and encouraged her to join him. When she sat down beside him on the edge of the bed, he kissed her lightly on the lips.

Immediately, without touching her in any other way, he began a dedicated verbal seduction the likes of which she had never imagined, much less heard before.

She merely murmured answers, thoroughly distracted as she watched, fascinated by what he *was* doing. His hands were not plying their magic on her body tonight. They were systematically manipulating the listening device he had removed from the back of the lamp base.

He made a particularly lurid suggestion and right in the midst of a word, snapped a small wire. "There. These inexpensive gadgets are so prone to malfunction," he said with grin.

Then he reassembled and replaced the instrument exactly where he had found it. "Now we can speak freely."

She stared at the base of the lamp, glanced around the room, then looked at him and whispered, "You are that certain?"

"I've been over the room inch by inch. This is the only one in here. It will be tomorrow before they can replace it, if they even bother."

"No one could have known *we* were coming here. Why would there even be these things?" Solange asked. "They had to have been placed here before we came. No one has been inside these rooms but you, René and myself."

"Yes, the mikes have been here for a while now. They're cheaply made and aren't even close to the latest technology. Chari probably outfitted every room in the house with them before beginning this. That way he could monitor any private conversations among those he hired to work here."

He eyed the gadget, then winked at her. "You never know who might be working for whom these days."

Solange looked down at her bare legs and tugged René's T-shirt down to cover as much of herself as possible. She suddenly felt very exposed. Jacques was still fully dressed.

"Did I shock you? I'm sorry. You know all that I said was for Chari's benefit. Hopefully, he'll believe we were so…busily engaged, we could not possibly have been thinking about destroying that toy."

She smiled and shrugged. "He might replace it just to see what you have to say to me next time. *I* would."

Jacques laughed. "It's good your sense of humor's in working order."

"A defense mechanism, I assure you. Nothing feels

terribly funny at the moment. I take it I need not honor my promise of a massage?''

He sighed. "I think it would be wise if we skipped that. I'm not sure I could bear another night like the last one.''

She frowned. "I regret you found it so difficult to endure.''

"Yes, well, *you* try sleeping when all you can think about is making love to the person in the next room.''

"I did," she said, looking up at him from beneath her lashes.

Again he laughed, a soft gravelly sound that did things to her inside. "Let's not go there, all right? As much as I'd love to, we have too many details to work out and very little time." He paused, reaching out to trail one hand down her arm as if he couldn't help himself.

"Then we should begin working," she said, her voice a bit sharper than she intended.

His laughter had died away and his dark eyes smoldered as they stared deeply into hers. "From now on you must act as if I have you completely in my power. That your one objective in life is to please me. You are a very independent woman, Solange, and I realize it goes against your nature, but it might be the only way Chari will believe you'll become involved in the work here. Will you be able to pretend this subjugation convincingly?''

She pulled her hand from his and got up from the bed, turning her back to him, chafing her arms with her hands, feeling chilled. "I hope so." Then she faced him again, biting her lips together. He was standing, too, now. Too close.

"You're afraid?" he whispered, putting his arms around her. "So am I, Solange. I'm afraid for you."

He remained quiet for some time, just holding her.

Then he seemed to come to a decision. "Please don't worry. Tonight I'll take care of everything. By tomorrow it will be over."

She realized what he meant to do, simply because she had betrayed doubt in her acting skills. He would kill them all in the dead of night. And there would be no way to gather the intelligence both their governments needed so desperately.

She pushed away, resolved to go through with the original plan. "No, Jacques. It's too soon. You will not sacrifice half of this mission because I had a fleeting moment of cowardice."

"It's not cowardly to be afraid, Solange."

"Well, it certainly is if you do not face those fears, is it not? My decision is made. We will do this. Can you not see? We *have* to succeed!"

He blew out a sharp breath and shook his head. "Then you have to promise me if you ever get into that lab, you'll be extremely careful."

"I am not a fool, Jacques. Nor am I inept."

He gave her an apologetic smile. "Sorry, I know that. When Chari speaks with you about doing it—and I'm almost convinced he will—keep in mind the motive we decided on."

"That I am entranced by you. Will do anything that you suggest?" She gave him a wry, deprecating smile. "What a typically male delusion."

"It was the only thing I could think of that he might believe," he explained. "He thinks I'm as mercenary as he is and he knows I want you. So he expects me to brainwash you into helping with his little project. If you simply volunteered, he would immediately suspect—''

"Yes, I do see your point. It would seem the most logical scenario, especially to a man such as Chari, I suppose." She hesitated before continuing, "I think it might be easier to pretend if…" She couldn't simply say it outright.

He stroked her arm again, a feather light caress. "If we *were* intimate?"

Slowly she nodded, risked leaning closer so that her mouth was only inches from his and closed her eyes.

The expected onslaught did not happen. Instead, he brushed her lips lightly with his. And again, the pressure was a mere touch. His hands cradled her upper arms, slowly drawing her closer.

"Come back to bed. Let me hold you," he whispered.

Solange went with him, lay next to him, amazed how natural it felt to be embraced by a stranger. She had never felt this comfortable in a lover's arms. But Jean had never simply held her this way, stroking her hair, her back, his lips pressed to her forehead. What incredible warmth.

That warm feeling soon escalated into heat that suffused her body. His, too, she noticed. She realized he did not intend to make any further advances without encouragement. The next move would have to be hers.

She raised her head and sought his mouth. Still his kiss remained gentle. Her hand wandered down his chest, toyed with the buttons. His fingers quickly covered hers, halting them.

"Jacques?" She breathed his name.

"This is a time out of time, Solange. Fear makes strange bedfellows," he murmured.

"I think I do not mind how strange you are," she said, smiling against his lips, pulling her hand from beneath his and sliding it inside the gap where one button had slipped loose. His skin was on fire, his heart thundering beneath her palm.

He wanted this as much as she did. Why was he holding back?

"No protection," he answered her unspoken question with a heavy sigh. "You could become pregnant."

"I am protected from that," she assured him. There was always a danger of rape in her work, both at the prison and following the late hours she often worked at the hospital. "And I am not promiscuous," she added. "There is no danger to you."

"What about danger to you?" he asked, a note of humor in his question. "You think it's wise to trust me this far?"

"You already hold my life in your hands, Jacques," she said honestly. "I do not believe you would put me at risk if you were not sure you were well."

He kissed her again, this time with unguarded passion, a sweet, hot invasion she welcomed with a moan of pleasure. No sooner had he ended the kiss than he began another, angling it differently, devouring her mouth with a greediness that proved contagious.

She kissed him back, sliding her hands through his hair, cradling his head as she demanded and offered, took and gave. His deep growl of encouragement had her moving closer to him, pressing her breasts into his chest, seeking contact with his lower body.

He crushed her to him, one hand at the base of her spine, the other firm against her back. He turned them, lying beneath her and tugged the hem of her shirt. She raised her arms and he pulled it off, pausing a moment, worshiping her with a hot gaze. "Magnificent," he breathed the word, then tasted her.

She cried out, a plea for more until he silenced her with his mouth again. Her fingers were already at his buttons, while his worked lower to get rid of the rest.

Suddenly there was nothing between them but a desire so heady and magnificent it could not be denied. His hand found her and plied the most amazing magic.

Solange reached for him, stroking in time to the way he touched her. All too soon, her body began to tremble, then quivered violently with release. He pushed into her with a force she had not expected and she came undone. One thrust and he held her still, his grip intense, his breath suspended. The tremors inside her drew him deeper still and he surrendered.

She watched him reach the pinnacle, heard the flow of love words escape in ragged gasps, felt the heat of him suffuse her inside and out. Solange closed her eyes and held him, wishing the moment would never end.

Solange had never felt so close to anyone in her life. This man who feared intimacy so much. This spy whom she could not afford to love and would never love her.

Odd how she felt no regrets at all, she thought, as her arms refused to let him go. Perhaps she was the strange bedfellow here.

Eventually he disengaged their bodies. She tried not to protest, at least not with words.

"Are you all right?" he asked. A polite question any man of manners might ask a woman after an energetic bout in bed. No, she was not all right, but that hardly mattered, since her problem was in no way physical.

"Better than fine," she answered, trying to make her voice sound light and well satisfied. True, her body felt content for the moment, but her mind and heart begged

the question. This had been more than a quick tumble
to relieve stress.

No surprise if Jacques treated it as such. He might
even convince himself that's all it was if he was wiser
than she, which he probably was. But Solange both realized and admitted something had passed between herself and this man that could never be described as casual
sex.

"This is so wrong, Solange. You shouldn't even be
here. I could kick myself for letting you and the others
persuade me to let you come with me. And now it
seems I have compounded the error."

That should have made her angry, the words *wrong*
and *error,* but somehow it did not. He was not speaking
of their making love, and she knew it. He was very
concerned about her, and this new closeness had em-
phasized that. "It will be all right, Jacques," she said.
"I will do my best, you know that."

"I do know that." He buried his face where the curve
of her neck met her shoulder and kissed her there with
what felt like desperation. "I'll never forgive myself if
anything happens to you. This is too déjà vu."

"What do you mean?" she whispered, pressing her
lips against his temple, reveling in the slightly salty taste
of their recent exertion. "Tell me," she encouraged
when he remained silent. She could feel his heart thundering next to hers as they lay skin to skin.

"My wife. She took a risk I asked her not to take
and she…did not survive. Always, I believed if something like that ever occurred again, I would be more
forceful in trying to prevent a disaster. Now look at
what I've done."

He pulled back to gaze into her eyes with concern.
He brushed her hair from her brow and kissed her fore-

head. "Look at you. About to enter the lion's den with only a bit of serum for protection. And it might not even work with what's in there waiting for you."

"Your wife, she was doing the same work as you?"

He nodded, releasing a weary sigh. "Also with National Security, but in a different area. If only I had insisted she keep the position within the agency that she had when we married, she would be alive today. She volunteered for undercover assignments instead. On the second one, she was killed. Shot."

"Someone forced her to become something else? To do this more dangerous work?" Solange asked.

His half laugh was dry and humorless. "No, Maribeth was a strong-willed lady. She had her own ideas, and that was one of them."

"She was trained for what she did, then? She must have known the hazards involved," Solange guessed.

"Yes, she knew. But you know how youth is, believing itself indestructible."

"How young was she?" Solange asked.

"Barely thirty." He caressed her back, gently as if she were precious to him. "And you, you are a child by comparison."

She sat up, taking his hand in hers and looking down at him. "Jacques, she knew what she was doing and so do I. Whatever has happened and whatever comes next, you are not to assume the blame for the decisions of everyone else."

"I understand what you're saying. Really," he added when she looked doubtful. "In my mind, I know I wasn't responsible for what happened to Maribeth, but in my heart, I curse the weakness that let me give in to her and let her do what she wanted. And now I've caved again and here *you* are."

She smiled. "Ah, poor Jacques. God deliver you from women with minds of their own."

He smiled back. "You make me sound as sexist as Chari. Maybe you're right."

"No, never that," she said, lying down again and snuggling closer to him. "You loved your Maribeth and I will not say again that you should not feel guilt. It goes with the grief, I believe. Anyone who loves someone dearly and loses them must experience a touch of responsibility for that loss no matter how the death comes about."

"Possibly. I never thought of it that way."

"If she had died of…say, a heart attack or cancer, would you not flay yourself unmercifully, certain that you had missed seeing the symptoms leading to her death?"

The look of surprise on his face made her smile.

"I see this all the time in the course of my work," she assured him. "It is not at all unusual." Then she added a warning in her most professional voice. "If I meet with a bad end, you may grieve me for a while, but do not take credit for the choices I've made. It is my responsibility as much as yours to protect the public from plague and death. I have made an oath to do so to the best of my abilities, just as I imagine you have done. Do we understand each other?"

"I believe we do, and thank you, Dr. Micheaux." His tone was much lighter, as if he were teasing her. "Have you any more words of wisdom for this old warhorse?"

"Only a prescription for his relaxation under pressure," she told him, emphasizing it with an intimate caress she knew would bring the desired response.

"Take immediately for best results?"

"Take as needed," she replied with a kiss of encouragement.

He kissed her back, long and hard, his lips only straying from hers long enough to say, "I have never known anyone like you, Solange, a bright little sun in all this darkness. Keep shining, will you?"

Never in a thousand years would she admit how frightened she was of what might happen to her. Since she was a physician, she knew better than most what a horrid death she could be facing if the serum she had been given proved ineffective. But she would not allow Jacques to double the guilt he felt over not protecting the women he cared about.

He did care for her, Solange knew. And he had dearly loved the woman called Maribeth, the one who had gone boldly to her death in defense of her country.

It would not do to let him know how afraid she was to do her duty as a human being and a doctor. If she did and things went badly, he would see it as his sacrifice of her for the good of all by insisting she go ahead and do as she had promised. Or if he prevented her going because she was afraid, that would endanger hundreds, perhaps thousands, by ending the mission too early. Either way, he would carry a burden of guilt on those broad shoulders of his forever if he believed for a second this venture into the labs had been his idea alone.

She slid her hand into his, palm to palm and intertwined their fingers and drew on his courage. She must be strong.

With his free hand he idly caressed her ear, trailing his fingers down her neck and across her chest as she lay in his arms.

"Are you sleepy yet?" he asked, his voice laced with

the barest hint of wishfulness. If she admitted she was, he would insist she go back to her own bed. If she had any sense, she would do just that.

"Not really," she heard herself saying. "Are you?"

Apparently not. He answered her with a kiss, this one in no way tentative, no way questioning, but the kiss of a lover who now knew precisely what she liked and wanted from him.

Though she thought very little at all while Jacques made love to her this time, Solange parted very reluctantly when the time came.

It was then she began to wonder whether she was making excuses, deluding herself. Perhaps it was only gratitude for the comfort he offered that she was feeling. The afterglow of sex with a proficient lover like Jacques could be deceptive, she supposed. How many other women had fancied themselves falling in love with him? Hundreds, no doubt. She seriously doubted she would be the last.

That must be it. Only when they lay together could she focus on something other than the real reason for their being here.

Back in her own bed in René's room, she could not sleep. Her dread of a meeting with Chari about the lab work grew greater with every hour that passed.

And, too, René had grown incredibly restless during the night. When morning came, Solange finally had to grant him permission to get quietly out of bed. They spoke briefly, both fully aware that every word they said was being picked up by the microphone in his room.

René's father had not been in to see him, nor had he asked for her to report on his son's condition. There was nothing wrong with René now but soreness in his bruised side and, of course, in his heart. Chari had clearly broken that beyond repair.

They never spoke of it in any detail, even in the short conversations they engaged in where they could not be overheard.

Jacques had interviewed René yesterday at some length in the other room that was no longer wired. Solange had not been present, but only because she was too busy keeping watch at the door to warn them if anyone approached.

Jacques had discovered that René was only aware of what they had known coming in, that there was a lab within the chateau. And that Chari had ordered a supply of the necessary materials for a formula similar to ricin, a protein toxin, a cellular poison.

While the toxin was not practical for use as a weapon of mass destruction in warfare, it could be one that might cause absolute terror and death on a smaller scale. It could not be transformed successfully into an airborne agent. *Yet.*

This morning she had conducted another brief conversation with the boy. She had felt the need to explain to René the pretense of her affair with Jacques. He did not need to know it was not really a pretense. She wasn't certain he believed it was a ruse, anyway, but he conceded it was necessary.

So far he seemed willing to do almost anything to stop what his father was doing.

Night had not come soon enough to suit Jack. All day he had thought of nothing but Solange. This was not a good thing, considering their purpose for being here.

Now they lay together again like lovers with nothing

more to think about than how to please each other next. It made no sense that he, steeped as he was in the importance of his job, would permit a diversion like this to happen. But here he was.

The tenderness he felt for Solange surprised him. Usually he went for the gutsy, competitive type he knew could hold their own in any situation. Like Maribeth. Maribeth had been fiercely independent, her courage flamboyant, her attitude of invincibility unwavering. And unrealistic, too. Loving her had proved mentally exhausting. He couldn't recall a single peaceful, quiet minute in all the time they had been together.

Solange seemed so gentle by comparison. She had courage all right, but it was tempered with logic and caution. She was a giving person, compassionate as well as passionate. He felt guilty comparing the two women, but their differences were so marked, how could he not?

He couldn't recall ever approaching a woman who seemed the least bit delicate and vulnerable.

Now he found himself wanting to know about this one, what made her tick. He wanted to learn how he could best protect her and keep that core of childlike innocence alive in her. This whole experience would change her radically, and more than anything, Jack did not want it to do that.

"Did you always want to be a doctor?" he asked, stroking her arm with his fingers. Her skin was so smooth, so fine textured and perfect. So pale and translucent. He could trace the small blue veins in her wrist, in her temple.

He leaned closer and kissed her shoulder, loving the little intake of breath that told him she liked what he was doing, that she was remembering what he had done before.

"Not always," she admitted. "I loved ballet when I was young."

"I should have guessed that. You move like a dancer," he told her, inhaling her scent deeply. It was like a drug. A truth serum maybe. He couldn't seem to stem the flow of words. "Grace and beauty in motion. Your hands fascinate me."

He took one in his and played with her fingers. Graceful, yes, but capable, too. These hands saved lives, provided care, did wonderful things for people. And for him. He pressed her palm to his lips.

She sighed and cuddled closer. Had he ever felt any closer to a woman in his life? If he had, he couldn't remember it now. She filled his mind, his memory and made him wish for things he should have learned never to wish for.

Jack knew he was in big trouble here. He was feeling things he knew better than to feel, and it wasn't all physical. Not by a long shot. But he couldn't pull away.

He couldn't seem to form any words that would set them firmly back into their roles. He was the operative here. She was just an agent of opportunity, recruited to accomplish what he could not on this mission. He was supposed to use her, not fall for her like a jumper with no chute.

"I love to dance," she said softly. "Tell me, do you dance, Jacques?"

"Like Baryshnikov," he growled, making her laugh.

God, he loved her laugh. It was breathy and soft. Sweet. It made him think of a sudden breeze on a still, hot day. Subtly surprising him with a pure, feel-good ripple that defied description.

It made him want more. *She* made him want more.

"I wish we were somewhere else," he said honestly.

"I wish we had met on vacation somewhere interesting."

"We would be tourists," she said, immediately picking up on the game. "You would ask me to come with you for a drink. Something dreadfully sweet with a small umbrella in it, perhaps. I would abandon caution and have two."

"And then dinner," he added, "and dancing after. I would hold you in my arms and hope you would agree to come to my room with me or ask me to yours."

She sighed again and tucked her head under his chin. "You would ask me where I was from, what I did." She fell silent for a moment. "And I would ask you the same questions. What would you tell me?"

"Lies," he admitted. The word was reluctant, gruff. "And after we parted, I would follow you home from wherever we had met."

"Why?" she asked, drawing back so that she could look at him with an expression of curiosity.

He kissed the frown off her brow. "Because I would want to know you, really know you in the setting you have made for yourself. I would want to explore who you are and become close enough so that I could tell you the truth."

"A lie or a line? I wonder."

"Let's call this truth of the moment," he replied.

"Yes, fantasy," she whispered. "Isn't it wonderful?"

"Maybe it could become real," Jack said. "When this is over, I might like to see if it could, would you?" Why had he said that? What was he thinking. He wasn't into lines or into lies. He never lied to his women. But was it a line or a lie?

"Perhaps I would *like* to," she admitted. "But as you

said, this is time out of time, Jacques. You and I are so…very different.''

When he said nothing to that, she added, ''But it is nice that we have one another now, tonight, isn't it?''

''As understatements go, that's a real winner.'' He *would* follow her and see where this led. He knew he would, because he would be powerless to stop himself.

He figured there must be magic at work here because he had lost the power to reason. If he had any good sense left, he ought to be backpedaling like crazy. He needed to leave himself a way out of an entanglement when all this was over. Even if he wanted more, he knew he couldn't…

The power of her embrace intensified. ''I think we should not plan beyond our time here.''

Maybe because she had said it first, Jack experienced a burning desire to plan like mad. Find a way to have her for as long as this lasted. And to make it last as long as he possibly could. It was crazy.

She was absolutely right. He was the one losing sight of reality here.

''Then we will make this time count,'' he assured her.

They would make love again. Later, when his blood had cooled, would be a better time to think beyond the mission to what might happen next.

Chapter 6

Solange chafed at captivity. She absolutely hated the lack of freedom. They'd been here three days and nights, and still Chari had not approached her about what he had mentioned—her helping in the laboratory. Without the information she might glean there, Jacques and his people dared not proceed. How much longer could this go on?

Her emotional defense against Jacques Mercier was as thin as the old shirt René had given her to sleep in. She had gone back to Jacques's bed last night.

She sensed he also had reservations about becoming more closely involved. And why would he not? There was no hope for a future relationship for the two of them. They were from different countries, different life-styles, different everything.

The overpowering attraction that existed between them, plus the on-edge tension of the wait and the knowledge that death lurked all around them made each

hour they spent here pure heaven or hell. There were
no in-between times. No relief.

"Mercier..." Chari obviously wanted to ask something, but hesitated. Finally he heaved a sigh and turned
away from Jack to peer out the window into the darkness. "Has René spoken to you since the escape?"

"Hardly at all. He sleeps a lot and is far from well."

"Were any of his injuries...permanent?" Chari asked
softly, playing the part of concerned father. Or maybe
some of the concern was real.

"No, I think he will recover from them, but they were
substantial," Jack answered.

This was the first time Chari had indicated much interest in the boy. Even now he did not seem nearly as
distressed as a father ought to be.

Jack wondered whether he was really inquiring after
René's health or just wanted to know how much he had
told Jack about what was going on here.

"He is able to walk now?"

Jack nodded. "Yes, a little. The doctor feels he could
use some sun and fresh air. As you might imagine, Baumettes was very dark and depressing."

For a long time Chari did not reply. Then he faced
Jack again. "The doctor may walk him in the back garden for a time tomorrow. You are to go with them."

The thought of getting out of the chateau, perhaps
finding a chance to slip into the woods and locate that
cell phone appealed to Jack. "I'll keep a close eye out.
Depend on it."

Chari merely nodded, then with a flick of his hand,
dismissed Jack for the evening.

"We are being closely watched from the rooftop,"
Solange commented as she looked past René at Jack.

"I do not know where they think we could go even if we decided to run."

Thank goodness Chari had given his permission for them to take René outside. They had only been out for a few minutes and already she had brightened considerably. Jack was so glad he had put in her request last evening during his talk with Chari.

"This garden could be beautiful," she said brightly, "but it certainly needs a bit of work."

"It was my grandmother's pride," René said, valiantly limping, pretending he was allowing Jack and Solange to support him in his weakened state. "The roses were magnificent when I was little. Now look at them."

Jack was too busy examining the high stone walls that encircled the place. The only way in or out of this enclosure was over the wall or through the spiked iron gate at a right angle to the kitchen entry. Two well-armed sentries lounged there on the steps.

"There were glass doors just there," René said, nodding at a stack of rough stones stacked nearly eight feet high against the back wall of the chateau. "The main ballroom opened into the garden. My grandparents gave a wonderful party here once when I was small." He looked sad.

"Perhaps one day you will have another party when this place is yours," Solange said with a smile. "Are you tired, René?"

"Not at all, but I suppose I should pretend that I am. We could sit over there, on the stone bench."

They walked him over and he collapsed on it with a touch of drama.

Jack remained standing, still observing their surroundings. Solange stood, too, as she spoke to René. "Lie down full-length and enjoy the sun. We will stroll around a bit."

She took Jack's arm and walked with him around the weed-choked gravel path. "What are you thinking?" she asked.

Jack shrugged. "That the place is as well defended as any castle of old. All it needs is a bloody moat and drawbridge."

"But your people could have taken possession of it easily enough, I do not doubt."

"Yes, we could have stormed it and cleared out this entire nest of vipers and their deadly venom. But we want the people they are dealing with.

"Even if we took some of these people alive, torture is outlawed. They would know better than to reveal anything. French prisons where they would go are two-thirds full of Middle-Eastern immigrants, a good number of them with strong ties to terrorist groups."

"Like Baumettes."

"Yes." He stopped walking and turned to her. "Knowing that, why do you risk your lovely neck working beside your father to treat prisoners?"

"My brother was one of them," she admitted. "The charges were false, of course." She laughed bitterly.

"Of course they were," he agreed.

"Yes, they all say that, do they not? But in my brother's case, it was the absolute truth. He died in prison before his case ever came to trial. Lack of prompt and proper medical care caused his death." She sighed. "He was so much like René, young and frail."

"You are very brave," Jack told her. "I admire you for it."

She blushed and ducked her head. "No, there you are

wrong. My courage is all feigned. And at the moment I am terrified this will be the end of me.''

She looked up at him, her eyes blue fire. ''But I want these people stopped, Jacques. They must be stopped. If there is anything at all worth facing death for, this would be the thing. I think of the terrorist attacks in your country and in other places around the world.'' She shook her head sadly. ''This could be much worse than anything we have seen.''

''And much closer to home,'' he guessed.

''Yes, but that does not matter. If they planned to terrorize even the smallest, most insignificant country, one I have never even seen on a map, I would still want to do this, Jacques. I am sworn to save lives whenever and wherever I am able. I thank you for allowing me to help you. We may save hundreds, even thousands.''

He held her hands in his, pressing them gently. ''We will almost surely have to take lives before this is over. How will you feel about that?''

''Sad. But I am not so naive that I cannot understand the necessity of it. Do what you must, Jacques Mercier, and help me to know what I must do.''

He only nodded in answer. As fragile as Solange seemed to be, Jack knew she had a core of tempered steel. In that respect, at least, she was much like Maribeth had been. Righteous, determined and courageous. No matter how much Solange denied it, she was brave.

But she was also untutored in this line of work, wholly unprepared. It scared the hell out of him how unprepared she was for it.

How much guiltier was he going to feel if he lost her the way he had lost his wife, a woman who was as competent and well trained as any agent he had ever known?

He had loved once and lost. Jack had made up his mind he would never put himself in that position again. But he was half in love with Solange already.

If he didn't distance himself from her emotionally, get to a place where he could view her as only a player in this game, he wasn't sure he could go through with the mission.

Several times now, he had been ready to halt the entire operation because of his fear for her. She was screwing up his priorities.

He let go of her hands and stretched his arms above his head as if to work out the kinks of his recent inactivity. If only he could let go of his feelings for her that easily.

"You lend me strength, Jacques," she whispered, her soft voice seeping through the strong walls he had built around his heart.

During the hour they spent in the garden, she and Jack discussed other inconsequential things. Idle conversation that might have been overheard by Chari himself without any consequences if he'd had any way to listen in.

Jack often found himself smiling at some of the stories she related about medical school. Making it through had not been easy for her, but she had dealt with all of it, employing her finely tuned sense of humor and the shrug of fatalism native to the French.

He reciprocated, unwilling to give her the silent treatment when she was so effusive.

"And so, we broke our glasses in the fireplace to seal our vow and went out to conquer the world with a football. Only we were too hung over to score the next day," he concluded, sharing one of the sillier episodes that took place during his prep school days.

She laughed merrily, as if they weren't confined in a quarter acre of weeds guarded by machine guns. Her resilience amazed him.

"Were your parents strict?" she asked.

Jack smiled at the memories that question brought. "Not at all. I was a free spirit and ran a bit wild. Dad is a doctor, an internist. My mother was a teacher. High school French. She does a lot of volunteer work now. They were both always so busy, they sort of left me to my own devices. I loved it."

"You were very popular during your school days, were you not? A 'hail fellow well met' as the English say?"

"A loner, always," Jack admitted. "I had many friends, yes. But I found it difficult to exchange anything of much importance with them. I guess you might say they were more like acquaintances."

"You were married," Solange said gently. "Your Maribeth, surely she was a close friend."

Had she been? Jack thought about it, then shook his head. "I suppose she was in a way. There were still things we never shared. We were a lot alike. Same background, same education, same training, same job."

"Much in common," Solange observed. "An excellent basis for a marriage. More important than love, I believe."

"Do you?" Jack asked, increasingly interested in what she thought about that. "And you, Solange? Have you ever taken the plunge?"

She smiled sadly. "No. Not into marriage, not even into love. Once upon a time I thought I might have both, but it was not to be."

"What happened?" Jack asked, drawing her down

onto a bench at the opposite end of the garden from where René lay sleeping in the sun.

"We simply did not suit," she told him. He could see the honesty in her eyes. And also the hurt.

Whoever the man was, whatever he had done, Jack had a sudden urge to throttle him. "Tell me his name."

Her eyebrows rose, and she smiled hesitantly. "Why would you want to know?"

Jack smiled back. "I would like to thank him for being the idiot that he is. Otherwise I might never have met you. No husband in his right mind would have allowed his wife to work in a prison hospital. To tell the truth, I'm shocked that your father allowed it."

Her sudden frown and tightening of lips told Jack he had made a serious faux pas.

She drew in a sharp little breath, and when she spoke, her words snapped like firecrackers. "How many times must I tell you? I make my *own* decisions."

He couldn't argue with that. "So you do," he said, nodding emphatically. "Some of them questionable, but firm and unshakable. I can certainly vouch for that."

She got up from the bench and started across the garden, her stride that of a woman with purpose. That's what she was, delicate or not, a woman with purpose.

That thought reminded Jack that he had an assignment of his own to complete, one in which she had virtually blackmailed him into including her.

There was nothing he could do to get her out of it now, short of sacrificing the most important aspect of it.

She had become way too important to him already, a serious distraction he could not afford, yet one he couldn't possibly ignore.

* * *

Solange found it impossible to remain angry with Jacques. She knew he worried about her safety and could hardly resent his concern. If only he would stop talking about it, perhaps she could forget it herself for a few minutes.

It did bother her that he seemed to think she was helpless, little more than a millstone around his neck. But then, men generally did underestimate her because of her appearance.

More often than not her deceptive fragility had proved an advantage to her, but she wished Jacques could look past that and be different.

In so many other ways he was vastly different. There was an awareness, a core of supreme self-confidence, a quality that not only invited but demanded trust.

René obviously admired him. She could see it clearly every time the boy looked at him. Even Chari had begun to confide in Jacques. That quality was a valuable weapon when he wished it to be, she realized.

She spent what was left of the afternoon reading. René had quite a collection of paperbacks, mostly adventure novels. It seemed he was a great fan of Ian Fleming, whom Solange had never before had time to read. It amused her to cast Jacques in the role of Fleming's hero.

If only his heroines were not so interchangeable, she thought with a grimace.

"What is the matter?" René asked her. "You do not like that one?"

Solange smiled at him. "Yes, of course. It's fascinating. I must admit your taste in books surprises me, René. Given your interests, I would have guessed you would choose something different, biographies of famous artists or the like. Perhaps the classics."

He shrugged his shoulder and closed the dog-eared novel he had been reading. ''These were Father's. I appropriated them from the rubbish bins when I was much younger.''

His grin took on a gleam of mischief. ''I used to play at being a spy for France, as Bond was for England. I discovered all manner of secrets about my teachers, though it was more of a personal nature than political.''

''What a scamp you must have been. I wonder they didn't ship you home from school.''

The gleam in his eyes died and he ducked his head. He said nothing.

Solange noted the sad vulnerability in the set of his slender shoulders. Though he did not say anything in response to her teasing, she guessed precisely what he was feeling.

He had no mother, had lost both the grandparents who loved him, and Chari had sent him away when he was still very young. Holidays home from school must not have proved pleasant.

He had created for himself a fantasy life where he was considered vitally important.

Could it be that he had fabricated this tale of the toxin and reported it to the authorities to exact a bit of revenge? Could his father merely be a paranoid recluse who hired armed guards to protect his privacy?

However, that would leave unaccounted for those odd shipments of supplies. Those purchases had been verified by outside sources after René had informed the authorities. Also, there was obviously a laboratory in operation on the premises. Chari had already admitted that.

No, René had not lied.

She would find the extent of his truth soon enough.

Jacques had assured her that Chari wanted her to assist in some way with the research.

What if she turned out to be as helpless as Jacques feared she was? She had never done anything like this before in her life.

Solange looked down at the book she held in her hands and fanned through the pages, watching as they riffled past her thumb.

Was she, like René, attempting to create a fantasy life of her own by forcing her way into this dangerous intrigue?

One thing she did know: there would be no closing of the book for a break on this one until it was over. And the resolution was in no way guaranteed.

And another thing to consider: loving James Bond never boded well for the heroine in the long term. In his next adventure there was always a new one.

Chapter 7

That evening after their walk in the garden, the atmosphere changed. It was almost as if the air held an electrical charge, a warning that lightning was about to strike.

This was it. Jack never discounted the revved-up feeling he always experienced when things were about to break or at least take a very important turn. Chari had called him in for another private talk.

He hoped he was right that this would be a turning point, because the waiting around was taking its toll on him as well as Solange, even more so since they had made love.

That had been a gigantic mistake on his part, thinking he could use that to calm her. Maybe release a little tension himself at the same time.

In her eyes he could see her confusion as clearly as he felt his own. Something more had happened in that bed than sex between two people who needed it.

But that was a problem they would have to resolve later. There was too much going on to deal with it now. Even if they had the time, they didn't have enough distance to think logically about this.

"It is crucial that my work here remain totally confidential," Chari was telling Jack now. "This is why no one other than Piers is allowed outside the chateau unaccompanied. Him I know I can trust."

Jack had not asked about the enforced seclusion. Chari was beginning to volunteer information. This was good, working exactly as Jack had hoped. It was almost a courting process, this drawing him out. If Chari played true to form, Jack would have all the details he needed in a matter of days.

They were having another of their little one-on-one chats over cigars in Chari's library. The mandatory summons had come just after supper.

The man seemed hungry for conversation, hopping from one subject to another, discussing current works of fiction, music and films. He touched on current events and politics, but only lightly, as if testing, feeling Jack out about his views on these topics.

Jack offered only observations, never conclusions. He purposely aroused Chari's curiosity with his own lack of opinions or questions.

Anyone coming into a situation like this would naturally be wondering what the big deal was; what the "research" Chari had mentioned Solange could help with was all about.

"Understandable," Jack said. "Security is essential to most creative endeavors." He tapped his ash and relaxed back into the leather wing chair.

Chari smiled and Jack smiled back. They might have

been two gentlemen farmers discussing the state of the weather.

The silence extended as they sipped strong coffee, puffed on the stogies and Chari waited for Jack to risk commenting further on the reasons for the isolation at the chateau.

He didn't. Chari expected him to be curious, to drag the story out of him about why all these extreme measures were necessary.

The windows were barred and all exits were securely bolted and welded shut except for main entrance in front and the door to the kitchens. Those were guarded both by cameras and guards working in pairs. No phones were in evidence anywhere, even here in the study that was Chari's private domain.

"Is the work to your liking?" Chari asked.

"Not taxing at all," Jack assured him.

It was true, he had found his duties light so far, mostly consisting of chores none of the others wanted to do, like making supply lists, doing a few loads of laundry and emptying trash cans. He knew the real task Chari had in mind for him would be eliminating the others once the boss had accomplished his scheme and got ready to break up housekeeping.

The whole setup was nothing like what French intelligence sources collected on them had indicated. Most of that consisted of erroneous assumptions constructed on appearance alone, and that, from a distance. They were all of dark complexion, well armed and looked like terrorists.

They were that, of course, but this was no politically based cell of hard-core believers out to abolish Western decadence. Jack didn't think any of Chari's hired men held any typically Middle-Eastern beliefs. Based on their conversations with each other and with Jack, they certainly had not been steeped in that culture.

Chari came closest to the profile, being half Iranian and half French, son of an expatriot from Tehran and a French journalist who hailed from Tournade.

René had filled in the gaps for Jack during one of their little talks. While working in Paris, studying at the Sorbonne, Chari and René's mother had married. She had already begun her career in film.

He had acquired a little notoriety when his movie had a controversial and rather dismal screening in Cannes several years ago. Though not a popular person in the film community, people did know his name. He had appeared in the news at the time.

Though it was not exactly public knowledge that he had returned to this particular house, his in-laws' old family home, he was reported to live in seclusion.

Nobody had minded that Chari was now a recluse until he had initiated what might be a very profitable hobby, one that had nothing at all to do with the movies. Now French intelligence, as well as select individuals working for the American Government, did mind. Very much.

"As I've said before, you possess qualities I did not recognize at first meeting, Mercier. You seem very confident. Certainly well educated. Piers says that you perform your assigned duties in an exemplary manner and have tendered some enlightening suggestions to improve security."

"This is not my first job," Jack admitted, but stopped short of offering any further information about himself.

"You have met the *others,* of course." Chari looked up and shook his head, his expression disparaging.

Again, waiting for, almost encouraging Jack to ask questions.

''Yes. And Piers is an excellent cook.''

He must be a professionally trained chef, in fact, given his habits in the kitchen.

Jack had overheard the guards called Todi and Edouard grumbling to each other in Italian. Vincent and Martin, who also paired off, rarely spoke to anyone else, but said enough that Jack had detected their sing-song island French.

These men were hired muscle from out of country, what the Europeans called guest workers, and—with the possible exception of Piers—obviously had no idea what they were protecting.

They didn't look scared enough.

Chari smiled again, sighing as he stubbed out his cigar and stood. ''The woman. Our little doctor. Did you find her agreeable?''

Jack nodded, realizing he was about to be dismissed. He put out the stinking cigar and got up, preparing to leave as he answered. ''Quite agreeable. She is quiet, but that suits me.''

''Loud women offend me, as well,'' Chari agreed. ''However, I was inquiring as to whether you had determined if she would be willing to lend a hand to the research I am doing.''

Ah, the awaited invitation.

Jack simply nodded. ''She will do as I say. Her need to please is her greatest weakness.''

''Have you discovered whether she has any background in medical research?'' Chari demanded. He looked a little piqued, probably because he had not been able to listen in on the activities and conversations between Jack and Solange beyond that first, staged love-making session.

"A little experience, so she says. Before his retire-ment, she assisted her father in his laboratory. He was involved in a minor way with the experiments dealing with HGH or something similar. Human growth hor-mones useful in antiaging formulas, I believe she said. A sort of sideline for him." This lie would be hard to disprove even with a background check, Jack hoped.

"That will probably suffice. She will have to move into the tower when she begins," Chari said, setting up the opportunity for Jack to ask about that part of the house.

He didn't. "Then, so will I, if you want her to do what you say." Jack shrugged. "Or simply leave us where we are."

Chari tensed, his eyes narrowed, his hands fisted. "You dare issue me this ultimatum? Keep you together or else?"

"No, sir," Jack answered with only a slight touch of subservience. "But you see it is not just anyone, but *I* whom she wishes to please. It was your idea for me to exert my control over her. That I've done, and as far as I can determine, there is no other leverage available to gain her cooperation except her feelings for me."

Chari laughed, at ease again. "Not troubled with hu-mility, are you, Mercier?"

"Not in the least. So, do we move or stay where she can also tend your son?"

There were others who lived in the tower that Chari had declared off-limits. Based on what he'd observed, Jack figured there were at least two people living there, not more than three. These would be the brains Chari had hired to do the real dirty work. Chemists? Doctors? Scientists?

Jack could hardly stand to think of Solange being exposed to their company, much less the dangerous nature of their duties. He couldn't afford to dwell on that increasing fear for her or he would terminate the mission too soon. He almost had.

One thing he had verified: Chari's motive was not political or ideological. It was definitely greed. He had zoned in on almost as rapid a way to make a fortune as winning a national lottery. And the payoff would probably be similar to that.

The question was, to what degree had the venture succeeded? Had he made any sales yet? Did he have a supply of the substance stockpiled? And who were his contacts among the groups who might be in the market for it? Once all that had been determined, this place, its contents and everyone involved in the whole nasty enterprise would become history.

The trick was to keep Solange and himself alive long enough to make that happen.

"You will remain where you are for now," Chari said, gesturing toward the door. "Bring her here to me first thing after breakfast tomorrow."

Jack nodded.

"Have you no curiosity at *all*, Mercier?" Chari asked as Jack was leaving.

He turned and regarded Chari with a nonexpression. "None. Good night, sir."

It was ironic, almost to the point of being funny. Chari was dying to tell someone what he was doing, to brag about his scheme and how clever he was, how rich he was going to be. Jack was about to become that confidant.

He pulled his turn at watch, then returned to his rooms. Solange was asleep on her cot, turned away from him. How small she was, how vulnerable, he thought.

René met him at the door and was now urging him into the other room. The minute they were inside it, the boy demanded, "Are you really sleeping with her?"

Jack looked him squarely in the eye. "That is none of your affair, René."

"She is a good person. Why are you using her? I will not allow it!"

Jack sighed. He did not need this complication. "I care for her. I will protect her. So must you. We are in this together, René. You must trust me."

Chari's son treated Jack to a blatant look of disgust. At that instant the son wore all the arrogance of the father. The expression faded, replaced by resignation.

With a shake of his head, René left the room and trudged back to his bed. He sat on the edge and hung his head, looking powerless and dejected. And young, very young. After a few minutes he crawled back into the bed and turned away.

This was all Jack needed, a moonstruck, jealous teenager who could blow their cover wide open on a whim.

Solange entered Chari's study with great trepidation. If Jacques was right, she would be ordered to the laboratory, where this man was perpetrating an evil she could scarcely imagine. She could comprehend the motives of ideological terrorists, if not their fanaticism. But who in his right mind would make and sell the means to endanger an as yet-unknown segment of the population? And could she possibly find a way to stop him before that happened?

Chari's narrow-eyed look measured her as she approached his desk. She had tried to make herself look as professional as possible under the circumstances. She wore the same blouse and pants she had arrived in. She had washed them in the sink the night before, but had found no iron to press them. Her hair was neat enough, slicked back and tied with a shoelace she had found in one of the drawers in René's room. The absence of makeup didn't bother her. She rarely wore much, if any, and had no desire now to look more than presentable and competent.

She met Chari's eyes, hoping to project more boldness than she felt. He blinked, then looked away and fastened his gaze on Jacques. Solange wondered if she disturbed him somehow or if he simply possessed a dislike of women in general.

"Have you spoken with her about the work in the laboratory?" he asked Jacques as if she were not even in the room.

"Only briefly, but she will do as I wish," Jacques said as he slid his arm around her shoulders and gave her a possessive squeeze. "Won't you, darling? If we are to marry, we must have the funds to leave this country and make a life together somewhere else. Perhaps the Caribbean? You would love Martinique."

Solange looked up at him—adoringly she hoped—and forced her lips to smile. "That would be wonderful."

Aware that she needed to pretend her greed equaled his, she turned the vacuous expression on Chari. "I understand we shall be well compensated for my services. Jacques has mentioned you are doing research?"

"Sit down, both of you," Chari said, gesturing at the two chairs flanking the front of his desk. He sat behind it, leaning back in his chair like the lord of the manor.

"You realize, of course, that if you later decide to decline, doctor, I shall have to…send you away?"

There was no mistaking his meaning. He would get rid of her. And Jacques, as well. "I can hardly resume my former position," she said, "not after the escape. As you are aware, the police are looking for me, now that I have aided the escape of two prisoners. It would seem I must rely on your generosity."

"Just so," he replied smugly. "You are to assist in the laboratory. Our former auxiliary is no longer able to perform his duties, you see." He pursed his lips and tapped them with his finger, then continued. "He had…an unfortunate attack of conscience."

Her swift intake of breath had betrayed her shock at Chari's implied threat. Solange released it slowly and gave him a resigned nod to show she understood. "I assure you that is not a contagious condition," Solange told him.

He frowned. "Clever, aren't you? You would be wise to save that ingenuity and apply it to your lab chores. No one appreciates a woman who flaunts her intelligence."

Solange hung her head and slumped her shoulders, properly subdued. She wished she could shoot him. She, who had taken an oath to save lives. He had driven her to think this way.

At that point Chari rose from his chair and led the way to a door opposite the one they had entered. There he retrieved a key from his pocket and unlocked what appeared to be a newly installed dead bolt.

"Enter," he said as he stood to one side of the portal. When Jacques would have followed her to the staircase inside, Chari blocked him. "Join Piers in the kitchens, Mercier. I will meet you there in half an hour."

Jacques and she exchanged looks, his reassuring, hers probably terrified. So that Chari wouldn't see her fear, Solange quickly turned to face the escalier, its worn winding steps curving both up from the landing and spiraling down into the depths of what must be the cellars. "Which way?" she asked, placing her palm against the cold stone.

"Down," Chari replied, closing the door behind him and locking it.

He did not take her arm, as she feared he might. Instead he remained several steps behind her in the near darkness. Meager light sifted from the slit of a window at the landing they had just left, and she noted a weak yellow glow from the floor below that she thought must be incandescent. She took her time, braced with one hand and placed her feet carefully on the worn, ancient treads. A fall resulting in an injury could well end her chance at this. And her life.

They passed the next landing and the closed door that led off it and descended farther into the depths of the tower. The steps ended at another door, this one probably as old as the chateau itself, solid oak and banded with bolted iron strips. A *dungeon?* He reached around her and opened it.

Fluorescent light flooded the room. Solange squinted as her eyes adjusted, not surprised to find a fully outfitted laboratory.

Though not large, it appeared that no expense had been spared. The walls, floor and ceiling appeared to be insulated with a material that looked virtually seamless. A few small animal cages sat empty on shelves in one corner. There were two refrigerators, a metal centrifuge, machines for milling and drying, and what looked like a state-of-the-art microscope.

The lab came complete with a mad scientist. The man bent over the microscope was enormous, his girth spilling over the chair on which he sat.

"Dr. Belclair," Chari said softly. "I hate to interrupt you, but here is Dr. Solange Micheaux. She is to be your new assistant."

The fellow pushed back from the worktable and swiveled his chair around. He did not stand. Solange wondered if that was because his legs would not support his weight. She put his age at over thirty, less than forty. His lank brown hair hung in limp strands that looked like tired quotes around his red-rimmed pig-like eyes. The mouth that pursed in their direction had a liverish cast to the lips.

His naturally dark complexion appeared jaundiced even with abundant illumination of bluish white light. He merely grunted. Words seemed too great an effort for him.

"Dr. Belclair," she said acknowledging the introduction.

"If you would, please, show her what she is to do," Chari said. "She is only a physician, but if she can assist with the formula, perhaps you should allow it for expediency's sake. Otherwise, use her as you will."

Solange tried to conceal her shudder. She raised her chin and turned. "Thank you, M'sieu Chari. I am certain Dr. Belclair and I will get on famously."

His shoulders shook with a soundless little chuckle and he nodded once. "Then I shall leave you to him." He stepped out and closed the door, indeed leaving her alone with Belclair.

Solange shored up her courage and faced her co-worker. She figured she could outrun him if worse came to worst, and hope that he collapsed from the exertion.

Dr. Belclair released a sigh that was almost a whistle. Then he blinked owlishly and turned back to his microscope.

Her one objective now was to get the information Jacques and his people needed and get out of this cursed dungeon. ''What is it we are doing?'' Solange asked, moving closer to the table where he was working, but still keeping some distance between them.

''Manufacturing death,'' he muttered, his voice as laconic as his attitude toward her. ''Replace those petri dishes in the freezer,'' he ordered. ''Gloves and masks are just there.'' He inclined his head toward a cabinet that sat against the wall.

Solange decided not to give him the satisfaction of questioning his announcement of what they would be doing. Let him assume Chari had told her. She noted he wasn't wearing a mask. Either he must have a death wish or he really was as simple as he appeared at first glance.

She went for the supplies and outfitted herself, also picking up one of the folded white lab suits and putting it on. It hung on her small frame. The wine-red caduceus embroidered on the pocket was underlined with the name of the hospital from which it had been stolen. Swiss hospital, she thought, but wasn't sure. Was that a clue? She filed it away in her mind.

''I have some experience working with my father,'' she told Belclair. ''He was involved with human growth hormone research. I know this is incredibly different area, but perhaps I could help. Are you having problems with the formula?''

She decided she might as well pretend she knew more than she did about what they were doing here. It wasn't as if Belclair would trouble himself to discuss her with Chari except in the most cursory of ways.

He nudged a notebook that lay next to him. "Have a look."

Solange gingerly lifted the book, found a clear spot on the worktable and took a seat some distance away from Belclair.

With mounting horror, she read the neat hand-printed research notes. They were copious and very detailed. Another's handwriting appeared first, then ceased on the page dated two weeks ago and was replaced by what she guessed was Belclair's.

When she had digested as much as she could, a comment escaped. "This is not ricin. Or abrin," she added.

"Similar," he grunted. "But easier to extract. Safer, too."

Easier? Solange knew that ricin was made from extract of the castor bean. Perhaps not so easy to obtain. She had read that abrin was approximately seventy times more toxic than ricin and it was extracted from the fairly common rosary pea. "How so?"

"Local field available. No need to order. I use the Genquist plant."

"Are you are a botanist?" She tried to sound impressed.

He replied with a nod to her question. "And chemist."

Solange read on. Apparently he had developed this himself. Had Belclair approached Chari with the idea of marketing this toxin or vice versa? Could he be the brains behind Chari's project? Chari was a greedy opportunist. Belclair looked like a man with a mission.

Perhaps the motive didn't matter so much as how

long he had been working on it and how much success he'd had. That's what Jacques would need to know.

She skipped to the last few entries. The problem seemed to be stabilizing the substance's toxicity. It lost its viability when the temperature of the solution containing it rose above eighty degrees Fahrenheit. In this climate, it could be used much as ricin or abrin might. In hotter climes it would be useless.

"Why employ a solution at all?" she asked. "Have you found a way to use it aerially?"

Again he grunted, obviously impatient with her interruption of what he was studying under the scope. "No. Impractical. As for the solution, it needs moisture to incubate. Infant formula works for that, but any other liquid severely dilutes the efficacy. I am trying different viscous substances now."

She swallowed her terror and tried to sound curious. She was, but it was a horrified curiosity. She glanced at the empty animal cages. "How do you plan to test it?"

He said nothing but she could see his fleshy lips curve up in a secret smile as he bent over the microscope and adjusted the knobs.

She waited, but that secretive expression remained his only answer to her question.

Solange needed to get out of this place. It reeked of mildew mixed with Belclair's body odor and a faint hint of something that smelled like incense.

The quiet in the lab would have rivaled that of a tomb if not for the doctor's regular wheezing and the monotonous click of the minute hand on the wall clock. Panic had heightened her senses. She had to get it under control.

Scarcely twenty minutes had passed and it felt like

hours. She replaced the petri dishes as ordered and waited for Belclair to give her something else to do.

If she bombarded him with questions, he might become suspicious, but the sooner she got the information needed, the sooner this would be over.

"I wonder why Chari has not provided you more help with this," she said, trying to make it seem simply a casual observation.

"It seems he has," Belclair mumbled.

"Yes. Well, I see you're too immersed in what you're doing to show me everything now. May I wander around and become acquainted with the area?" she asked politely.

He merely shrugged, busy with an eyedropper, adding a minuscule amount of something to one of the dishes left in front of him. She watched him prepare another slide.

She kept on the latex gloves as she opened the first of two doors, the one that was obviously new and made of thick metal. It was unlocked. Inside on a stainless steel table were six small drums that would hold about two liters each. "What is this?" she asked.

He spared her a glance. "Incubation," he mumbled. "Close that door. That room's temperature controlled."

Before she complied, she noted the thermostat just inside, set at forty degrees Fahrenheit. The room looked even more heavily insulated and appeared to have a separate ventilation and cooling system.

"I suppose you have ricin and abrin, as well?" she asked. "For comparison?"

"Minuscule amounts," he said with a shrug of one shoulder. "Just you try buying rosary pea plants or a batch of castor these days. I had to purchase it already prepared. Damned difficult to do."

God in heaven, she hoped so. There should be a careful eye kept on that sort of product. It made a certain sort of sick sense that someone with an eye to profit would come up with something that would not be as suspect for making protein toxins like these. In this case, the plant he had mentioned.

But Belclair spoke as if he had done the purchasing himself, Solange thought. Jacques would need to know that. It could be very significant. It appeared more and more as if Chari were only the host here.

"Where are those samples?" she asked. "I would not want to cause a mix-up."

"Only on the slides. Carefully marked."

"Very efficient." She opened the other door, the wooden one. This room only contained a none-too-clean toilet and a rust-stained sink. Elsewhere she had not observed even a speck of dust. Apparently Belclair's penchant for absolute cleanliness did not extend to the toilet facilities.

Eventually, he abandoned his current testing and put her to work recording his findings. Thankfully, he showed no more interest in her than he did the rest of the equipment in the room. A means to an end, a recording device.

Why was he doing this? She burned to ask, to find out how anyone in his right mind could be so cold-blooded and engage in such deadly work.

His dictation was slow and laborious. Solange grew more hopeful as she recorded his failure and had plenty of time to think how she might exacerbate it indefinitely. Only she did not want to drag out the resolution to his experiments. She wanted to end them completely. *Now.*

Self-preservation urged her to race headlong up those

stairs, find Jacques and demand that he get her out of this place and away from these people by any means necessary. But a more logical and responsible part of herself realized it was her responsibility to do everything she could to put an end to the madness here.

Jacques trusted her to help him. She had to do something. But what?

Chapter 8

Jack finished his supper and pushed away from the table. He looked over at Piers. "I'll take the midnight watch."

"You will take the eight o'clock," Piers responded, looking at the kitchen clock. "You are on in five minutes."

It would do no good to argue. Though Jack needed to see that Solange was all right after her day in the lab, he exercised all the patience he possessed and went to the roof to stand lookout.

Tonight they had furnished him with a loaded weapon, a late-model fully automatic hand machine gun. Lightweight, effective and probably loaded with hollow-point ammo. He could sweep the roof with it right now and take out half of Chari's force. But then he'd be stuck up here until he starved or jumped, and Solange would still be in the tower. And Chari's plan would still go forward. He abandoned the urge.

In addition to the weapon, he had a simple walkie-talkie to communicate with the other guards. If he spied anything moving, he was to alert them.

But he also noted that, unlike on previous watches, there was no one monitoring the same area he was covering. They were now trusting him enough to keep watch alone on the territory he had been assigned.

Chari needed someone he could trust and talk openly to about what he was doing. The taciturn Piers must not be filling the bill. Jack was cultivating that need in hopes of getting the full inside story on the development of the toxin, who else was involved and how it had been, or was to be, employed.

For the next three hours he alternately paced the narrow ledge of the roof's overhang and rested against the dormer. That second tree taunted him, its branches beckoning in the moonlight, daring him to scale down the stone exterior of the chateau and retrieve his communication gear from the place where Eric had left it concealed.

The team must be wondering what had happened to him and Solange. Since he had not contacted them, would they mount an invasion? No. Eric would probably try to connect psychically first. The trouble was, Jack had no power to send or receive telepathically. None.

The best he could hope for was that either Eric or Joe would "see" him in one of their peculiar visions and know he was still kicking.

Out of sheer boredom and just in case they were really tuned in, he gave it his best shot. He closed his eyes and concentrated as hard as he could.

Okay, guys, I'm here. Still waiting on the informa-

Play the Lucky Hearts Game

and get...
2 FREE BOOKS
and a FREE MYSTERY GIFT...
YOURS to KEEP!

yes! I have scratched off the silver card. Please send me my *2 FREE BOOKS* and *FREE mystery GIFT*. I understand that I am under no obligation to purchase any books as explained on the back of this card.

Scratch Here!

then look below to see what your cards get you... 2 Free Books & a Free Mystery Gift!

345 SDL DZ5U　　　　　**245 SDL DZ6A**

FIRST NAME　　　　　　　　　　LAST NAME

ADDRESS

APT.#　　　　　　　CITY

STATE/PROV.　　　ZIP/POSTAL CODE　　　　　　(S-IM-05/04)

Twenty-one gets you
2 FREE BOOKS
and a **FREE MYSTERY GIFT!**

Twenty gets you
2 FREE BOOKS!

Nineteen gets you
1 FREE BOOK!

TRY AGAIN!

Offer limited to one per household and not valid to current Silhouette Intimate Moments® subscribers. All orders subject to approval.

*tion. Check on Solange, will you? If anything's wrong
with her, let's get her out of it. Now!*

The night remained still. Jack had an hour to go on
his shift. With a sigh, he paced some more, trying his
best not to imagine Solange's workday and what she
might have been exposed to.

The hour crawled by. Jack was just about to reenter
the door that led off the roof when something thunked
solidly against the roof not three feet from him. He
dropped and rolled, concealing himself in the corner
between the dormer window and the tiles. That threw
the object into relief against the sky.

An arrow? Jack almost laughed at the rudimentary
means of communication. Must be Eric's idea. He had
a quirky sense of humor.

After a brief glance around to see whether anyone
else had observed it, he crawled over and yanked the
missile out of the crumbling tiles. It looked like a bolt
from a crossbow. A small paper cylinder was wrapped
around it.

Jack stuck the entire thing inside his vest and got to
his feet. It was time for his shift to end. He only hoped
the message did not require an immediate answer.

At least one of the guys had come to check and would
now know he had not been able to retrieve the phone.
He raised one hand above his head as if stretching out
the kinks in his muscles and lowered it slowly. There
was a rapid blink from the woods near the tree that
stood sentinel over his cell phone. Might have been a
firefly. He smiled into the darkness knowing the firefly
could see him. Night vision equipment would have been
necessary to identify him on the roof.

The moment he returned to the room Solange and

René occupied, he realized she was not in there. Her cot was neatly made and empty.

The boy was awake and waiting for him. He grabbed Jack by the arm and urged him into the bathroom.

With the water running, he leaned close, his whisper desperate. "Where is she?"

Jack glanced into his own bedroom. His bed was still made, just as they had left it this morning.

René was already shaking his head. "She never came back here. All day she has been away! What has he done with her?"

"I'll find her," Jack promised. "Go back to your room and wait."

Dread turned him ice-cold. Somehow he had to figure a way to avoid the cameras placed so strategically around the chateau, get through Chari's study and into that tower.

Read the message. The thought bombarded him like a blow to the head.

Jack didn't even take time to question that. He immediately fished out the arrow with the small cylinder, removed the tape and unrolled the paper. The arrow bolt he replaced inside his vest. It could serve as a weapon.

The message was written in Cyrillic so Jack knew it was from Eric. *All is well. She is not afraid. Try this again. Got your drift, but concentrate more.*

Eric must have realized Jack would rationalize any telepathic reassurance he might receive as a product of wishful thinking. Absolutely right, he would.

This written message, however, was proof that Eric had received the earlier "transmission" Jack had attempted and was answering with what vibes he had picked up from Solange.

Jack ran the paper under the tap and washed off the ink, then flushed the paper down the toilet.

"She's all right," he told René. "I have word that she is all right and not afraid."

"Who sends you this word? Can we believe it?"

"Yes. I can't tell you who yet, but he is reliable."

Hell, he didn't even sound convincing to himself.

Could he trust that Eric's concern for Solange's welfare matched his dedication to the overall mission? Would he sacrifice her for the success of it?

Going out that door and getting caught on camera approaching Chari's private study could very well blow his cover to smithereens and Jack knew it. Chari would never buy the idea that Jack had so much concern for a mere woman that he would violate security.

He took a deep breath and tried to think rationally.

It was hard, damned hard to do. Hundreds, maybe thousands of lives depended on the success of this mission, he reminded himself. The possibility of endangering one person for the good of so many should not be such a difficult decision to make. Solange had volunteered for this, insisted on it repeatedly. She had known the risks going in.

Just as Maribeth had known, Jack thought with a shudder.

But if he ignored his own training, went rushing to Solange's rescue, what would the consequences be? If he found her safe and unharmed, he would have blown the mission for nothing. They would both be killed anyway, simply for not following Chari's rules. And if he found her…otherwise…that would also end things here and now.

There was nothing for it but to stay put and pray that

Eric was playing it straight with him, that Solange was all right. And not afraid.

It was going to be a very long night.

"Chari wants to see you," Piers told Jack when he arrived for breakfast.

Not half as much as Jack wanted to see Chari. With monumental effort Jack concealed his fury and went to answer the summons. He strolled down the corridor as if he had all the time in the world, trying his best to look uninterested for the cameras. Chari would be watching.

The welcome Jack received surprised him. Chari appeared almost apologetic. "Mercier, I did not send you the woman last evening. You must have been concerned that I had gotten rid of her." He paused, now wearing a look of anticipation. He wanted Jack to question him. When that didn't happen, Chari finally added, "Fortunately, that was not necessary."

Jack shrugged, assured now that Solange was at least alive. "I was too tired after my shift to think much about it."

Chari laughed and relaxed. "The fact is, I was too engrossed in my next project and forgot everything else. By the time I remembered she even existed, she had already let herself into one of the tower bedchambers and gone to bed." He turned his palms up in a helpless gesture and smiled. "She is back at work this morning."

Jack nodded. The best course of action right now was to avoid discussing Solange. His temper was hanging by a very slender thread. Was she really all right? Had she run into any problems? He knew if he asked and betrayed how important she was to him, Chari would use that to the max.

"I'll join her there tonight," Jack said.

"Ah...no," Chari said with a hesitant smile. "I think perhaps she might be...distracted by your company. Why not give her a few days to adjust?" He paused. "Then we shall see."

Jack glowered, unable to conceal his anger. He was almost as infuriated with himself for the lack of control. He was *always* in control. Hopefully Chari would think this lapse had to do with the deprival of sex.

In addition to the powerful urge to make sure she was unharmed, Jack needed to find out what she had learned. Who was he kidding here? He wanted to hold her and then to get her the hell out of that tower.

"That was not our deal," Jack grumbled. "I thought you were a man of your word."

Chari's dark eyes widened at the insult. He pressed a hand to his chest. "I am wounded, Mercier. Have I not allowed you to have her every night since you arrived? Surely you are not such a slave to your desires."

This was definitely a power play, Jack realized. "I missed having a woman when I was in prison. You said she was mine."

"She is still yours but I have a use for her now. Be patient, my friend. What I want her for has nothing in common with your needs."

The light of malice in Chari's eyes had dimmed and now looked more like worry. He was a man without any friends. Even Piers, the most loyal and informed of Chari's men, seemed to have nothing to do with him other than carrying out his orders. "If it will settle your mind, I will bring her to show you she's not been misused. How would that be?"

"A generous gesture on your part," Jack said, pretending to be mollified a little by the offer.

"A building of trust between us," Chari added with a smile that looked genuine.

Jack understood what Chari wanted. Interest. Admiration. It was time to concede a little. Not too much of the first, however. And only a glimmer of the last, just enough to prod Chari into revealing more of his plans.

"You would like to tell me about your project," Jack said, sounding only mildly interested. "May I sit?"

"Of course." Chari inclined his head to the wing-chair facing his desk, then sat down in the heavily carved, thronelike chair behind it.

His eyes lit up like neon over Vegas. "I am contacting everyone I know in the film-making industry and have begun collecting possible scripts. As soon as I settle on that one special property, something with truly universal appeal—"

"Not *that* project," Jack said, idly waving away the smoke that was making him nauseous. "The other. I know you do not have Solange doing correspondence and reading scripts in that tower of yours."

Chari sighed, his disappointment at being interrupted evident. "Oh, that. To put it succinctly, I am developing a biological weapon for sale. Rather, I'm having it done. You understand, this is no different from the invention of the Gatlin gun," Chari said with righteous conviction. "Merely another weapon."

Jack suppressed his scoff and schooled his features to remain slightly bored. "It could be considerably different as an airborne agent. Impossible to control, for one thing and dangerous to use. No one but Jehad fanatics would be interested and they are not reliable as paying customers."

Chari was already shaking his head. "No, no, it is not some flyaway cloud of major destruction. It is a topical substance, something like what is already available, only much safer to use. It might also serve to contaminate a limited water supply. That is what we are working on now."

He seemed very sincere as he continued to justify the venture. "These groups are going to use *something,* after all, and it might as well be this. The kill rate will be less than what they have, but it is the safety factor in dealing with it that appeals, especially to those who object to becoming martyrs." His smile was beatific, as if he were doing the world a favor.

Jack fiddled with his cigar for a moment, then looked up at Chari, who must be waiting expectantly for a word of congratulations. Clearly he believed he was only taking advantage of a money-making opportunity. "So you have buyers already?"

"Oh, yes, absolutely."

"It's risky. You would have done better to stick with regular arms sales."

It was Chari's turn to scoff. "You didn't fare all that well with those, now, did you?"

"Point taken," Jack admitted. "Are your clients reliable?" *Tell me who they are, you son of a bitch, so we can wind this up.*

"They have funded the project."

"Middle-Eastern?"

Chari laughed, leaning back in his big leather chair and puffing on his cigar. "At last I have you curious, no?"

"Concerned," Jack admitted. "If it doesn't work the way you say it will, guess who your clients will come after. This is a very small operation and you have damned little backup. I, for one, would not care to be around you if the stuff fails to provide the results they are after. Have you shipped any of it yet?''

Chari's sly smile grew hard. "Why? Planning to try to leave before the results are in?''

Jack nodded thoughtfully. "Maybe. Depends on who we're dealing with. If it's Bin Laden's friends or the PLO, I'm out of here. The IRA or the like, I could handle. I could reason with *them* if they're not satisfied.''

"How positively racial of you, Mercier. Reasoning is my area of expertise anyway,'' Chari informed him. "You need not *deal* with anyone at all. Except me, of course. And you *are* staying here, regardless.''

Chari still had told him nothing of any value in determining the amount of substance that might have been shipped, who had it or what they planned to do with it. He wasn't going to say, either. Jack had to find out before he rang the death knell on this operation.

As an answer to Chari's statement, Jack smiled and stood. "Well, if I'm hanging around, at least give me my woman back when you aren't using her.'' He managed a grin. "And do make sure she washes her hands, will you?''

Chari laughed, slapping his palm on the desk as he stood. "Ah, Mercier, your wit is dry. I do enjoy our conversations. Go now. I have work to do.''

Jack stopped at the door and turned, thinking he might as well try to create an opportunity to retrieve the cell phone.

"By the way, when I was on guard last night, I thought I saw movement in that copse of trees to the north,'' Jack said. He needed that phone out there and he intended to get it. Telepathy, while useful in some instances like last night, was certainly too unpredictable to employ when trying to coordinate a full-scale assault.

As soon as Solange emerged from the laboratory and furnished him with the information they needed, he intended to end this lark of Chari's once and for all. For that he needed the phone to make a definite plan for a concerted attack that wouldn't get them all killed, either by gunfire or biological accident.

"But you did not report this incident?" Chari asked, his voice deadly calm.

"I mentioned it to Todi when he relieved me at midnight. I expect it was only an animal stirring the brush."

Chari went to the window, pushed back the drapery and peered out for a few minutes. The window faced north. "Take Edouard and Piers with you. See if there are signs it was anything other than what you suspect."

"Now?" Jack asked. "Piers is busy."

"Do it!" Chari demanded, his uneasiness betrayed by the clenching and unclenching of his fists.

"Right away," Jack said. He ambled out and headed for the kitchen.

He would be taking a chance, going out there with the other two, but he had known Chari wouldn't trust anyone, especially the newcomer, out there alone. Jack had discovered that the only person allowed to leave the chateau alone was Piers, who went into Tournade occasionally for supplies. Or to make deliveries. That thought was chilling.

Eric would have erased all traces of his presence last night, so there would be no tracks to find. The problem was how to retrieve the phone without Piers and Edouard seeing him do it.

* * *

"The sun on my face feels good," Edouard announced to no one in particular as they strode across the clearing to the copse of trees.

Jack knew he had better take charge and give directions. "You begin over there and work back this way. Piers, if you would, start at that end. I will go in between you. Careful not to disturb any tracks you might find. If there are any, we might have to follow and see where they lead."

As soon as they separated, Jack went directly to the tree, toed the leaves away and found the small box immediately. Instead of crouching to retrieve it, he bent and pretended to look in several other areas around it. Piers seemed more intent on watching him than in checking for footprints. Edouard stood at the edge of the trees lighting a cigarette.

"You there, get busy!" Piers called out.

Jack realized it was the other man Piers had been observing, not him. He wandered back to the box, slowly crouched, scooped the items out of it and tucked them in his pocket. As he stood, he saw Piers headed his way.

Jack tamped down the ground over the box with his foot, then headed deeper into the trees, bent over and was examining the ground when Piers approached.

"Did you find anything?"

"This could be tracks. A large dog or something. I guess it was an animal, after all." He got up and started back to the clearing. Piers was just ahead of him.

Jack's heart nearly stopped when Piers halted by the tree where the phone had been. He watched the man stoop, rake aside dead vegetation with one hand and begin to lift out the box.

With a move that rivaled sleight of hand, Jack took out the phone and small set of lock picks and tossed them behind him into the brush. A split second later, Piers stood and turned on him. "The dirt has been disturbed. What is this?"

Jack shrugged. "Just an old bon-bon box. Looks like it's been there for years. Not important."

"It is empty," Piers agreed, but he wore a strong look of suspicion. Edouard had joined them by this time, darting expectant glances from one to the other.

Jack knew he was about to be searched. He moved forward, getting as far away from the ditched phone and set of lock picks as possible. Piers was now holding the box in one hand, his pistol in the other.

"What's the problem?" Jack asked.

"Search him," Piers ordered Edouard.

With a disgruntled sigh and roll of his eyes, Jack raised his hands. Edouard began patting him down expertly, making Jack wonder if the man had ever been employed by the police. Too late, just as Edouard reached his ankles, Jack remembered the crossbow bolt. He had tucked it in the top of his boot after he had dressed this morning.

Piers tossed the box down, stalked over and grabbed the bolt out of Edouard's hand the second it appeared. "This was inside that box?"

"No. I've had it all along."

"Not when you first came. Where did you get it?"

"Off the roof," Jack said honestly. It was always best to keep to the truth whenever possible. "It was stuck up there between the tiles. Probably for years. Makes a fair weapon, I thought, so I kept it." He smiled. "In prison one learns to appreciate windfalls such as that."

He was close enough now to disarm Piers. Edouard

had not drawn his weapon yet. It was now or never. He had to decide. If he killed both these men, he would play hell explaining it to Chari. And Solange was still locked in that tower with who knew what.

"We will see what Chari has to say about this," Piers said. As he spoke, he was glancing around them at the ground as if still searching for tracks.

Jack pushed past him, bumping his shoulder to divert him. "Let's go, then."

He headed back to the chateau, knowing they would have to follow. At least the bolt had drawn attention away from the box and what it might have contained. He had to hope Piers wouldn't return later and resume the search.

"Stay, Edouard," Piers commanded. "Have a closer look in this area. If you find anything, wait here. I'll be back as soon as I've taken care of this."

Jack almost groaned. He and Piers were in the open. It was too late now to do anything. He could probably escape, but he wasn't about to leave Solange in there. If he took anyone out at this juncture, it needed to be Chari.

Solange made and fetched the coffee. Suppressing her need to throttle the oversize egomaniacal chemist, she even did the housekeeping chores around the lab. But he would not allow her to help with what he was formulating. Even when she tried to cajole him with flattery, he merely brushed her aside and ordered her to do something else.

With time on her hands, she snooped without any guile at all since he was ignoring her. She found no written records of any shipments or lists of components stored. All she knew was what she actually saw, those containers in a temperature controlled room and petri dishes with cultures labeled with some sort of code.

After repeated attempts that first night to get someone to open the door that led back through the study, she had gone up the old stone steps and found an unoccupied bedroom. It had been used recently, probably by the fellow she had replaced—the one who had the attack of conscience.

The very thought of what must have happened to him gave her the shivers. She had hardly slept at all.

Now once again, after the noon meal, she climbed the stairs, her feet like lead weights, her heart the same. She paused and knocked, hoping Chari would be in his study and answer her, but there was only silence beyond the door. She continued up the stairway to the room where she had spent the last night.

How she missed Jacques. If only she could see him for a little while, have him hold her and reassure her. Even if he could do nothing right now to end all of this, he could at least lend her a bit of his courage to sustain her. She felt so isolated.

One had to wonder how he did this sort of thing for a living. Did he go from one mission such as this straight to another? She knew his bringing her with him was not his choice. Did he usually do this work in the midst of evil alone? How did he endure it?

She flopped across the bed and toed off her shoes, exhausted mentally, if not physically.

With a sigh, she whispered into the stillness. "Where are you, Jacques? What are you doing at this moment? Why do you not come for me?"

Just as her eyes were closing, the door creaked open. With a cry of surprise, she sprang upright. *Chari.*

His sly smile frightened her, but Solange was well

used to concealing her fright. It was the only way she had been able to face going to the prison to work with her father. Her effort had doubled during the two times she had gone without him. That practice came in handy now.

He was dressed casually, as he had been before, wearing chinos, a dark brown pullover, a canvas vest and boots. His features, like his son's, were nearly perfect, his body toned and fit. She realized that Chari was well into the role he had assumed and that he liked it.

"Yes? What do you want?" she demanded, glaring at him, realizing it was definitely the wrong question, the moment she asked. "Have you come to release me?"

"Mercier is restless. If I allow you back into the manor, can I trust you to keep your mouth shut about the research?"

She rolled her eyes, clutching her arms as if she were cold. "What could I possibly tell him?"

"Him? Anything you like, because he already knows. But do not speak to the others." His eyes narrowed. "Any of them, do you understand? And say absolutely nothing about the project to my son."

Solange sighed, her shoulders drooping in spite of her effort to appear strong. "I know nothing, anyway. All I have done thus far is housework. I have no clue what the research is about unless it is a cure for megalomania."

"Those are dangerous words, Doctor. Petulance is so unbecoming."

"I was referring to your so-called chemist," she said, understanding that if she angered him any further, he would not allow her to go to Jacques. "The man is a pig."

Chari relaxed, leaning back against the door frame and crossing his arms across his chest. "Yes, I must agree, but unlike you, he is qualified to do the work. You are merely there to assist him."

"I could do more, perhaps," she said, "if you bothered to explain to me what it is you intend and what you have already accomplished."

"Remember your place, woman," he warned in a silky voice.

"Then suppose you allow me to do what you know I am qualified to do and see how René is doing," she suggested.

"So, go," Chari said, with a nod to the open door. "No one is stopping you. I would have let you go last evening if you had waited awhile. I was occupied elsewhere and did not hear you if you knocked. When I finished, you had already come up here and retired for the night."

"I was to wait in the stairwell?" she asked. "It was a long day and I was too tired."

His lips stretched into a suggestive smile. "You are no beauty, but you did make a fetching sight curled on that bed." He glanced over at the rumpled chintz and shook his head, as if remembering. "I was almost tempted to stay."

Solange tried not to run as she headed out. His cruel laughter curled behind her in the stairwell.

Chapter 9

Once they were inside the manor, Piers ordered Jack to the study. Chari was not there when they entered.

"Stay here," Piers ordered, "and under no circumstances, touch that door." He inclined his head toward the tower. "Or anything else in the room." His glance cut briefly to the small camera mounted in the corner as if to remind Jack he would be watched. Then he left.

Jack remained standing as he waited to see what would happen next, but he couldn't help his gaze drifting to the place where he had last seen Solange. To his amazement the door opened. Chari stepped through and stood aside to allow Solange into the study.

"What are you doing here? Did you find something during the search?" Chari demanded of him.

Jack ran a quick assessment of Solange, who appeared to be holding up all right. She looked a little pale, but not all that frightened or ill. "Piers asked me to wait here. He went to find you."

''Why?'' Chari demanded. He took Solange by the arm as if she were a balky child and gave her a slight shove in the direction of the chair to one side of his desk.

She sat obediently, looking up at Jack, her eyes narrowed with concern. He wondered if it was for herself or for him. What had she done?

Before he could answer Chari, Piers came rushing back in from the other door, his face red with exertion. ''Edouard has gone. Disappeared!'' he exclaimed. Then he pinned Jack with a black glare. ''Did you tell him what happened?''

''No, he just came in,'' Jack said truthfully. This was getting more interesting by the minute.

Piers holstered his weapon, a good sign. Then he wiped his brow with the back of his sleeve. ''We found a weapon on Mercier, a crossbow quarrel that he says he found on the roof. I marched him back here to explain it to you and left Edouard to continue the search. When I returned, he was gone. There is no sign of a struggle out there. Nothing. I think he has run off.''

Chari had gone very still, his brow furrowed and his jaw clenched. ''Do you think he...knows?''

Piers shook his head. ''No, I do not believe so. How could he?'' They both looked at Jack, who simply shrugged.

Best-case scenario, Eric was out there somewhere and had captured Edouard. Not that the guard would be able to furnish the team any information about what was going on in the lab, but under pressure, he would most likely provide the day-to-day operations in the rest of the chateau. Or Edouard could have gotten tired of being confined to the place and decided to take a hike while he had the chance.

"Find Edouard and get rid of him," Chari ordered. Piers left immediately and Chari turned to Jack. "Now, about that crossbow quarrel."

"As I explained to Piers, when a man spends time in prison, he learns never to ignore a potential weapon. Many times it means the difference between living and dying. The old arrow was stuck there on the roof between the tiles and so I took it. Now you have it. End of story."

After a long, tense silence, Chari nodded. "Go about your duties, then."

Solange released an audible gust of relief that drew Chari's attention. He shot her disgusted look, then spoke to Jack. "I brought her up to show you she is well and thriving. Unless you want that to change, let us not have any further cause to question your loyalty, Mercier."

"No problem," Jack said. "Are you well, Solange?"

"I'm fine," she said, and started to say something else when Chari cut her off.

"Go back to the lab. *Now!*" he ordered.

She threw a helpless look at Jack who tried to reassure her without words. He hated like hell to see that door close when she left. Chari would lock it and she would be trapped for the day and possibly the night, too, after this incident. Jack knew things had to break, and soon.

Back in Tournade, the Sextant team was waiting for news. Eric Vinland had some for them. He stamped the loose dirt off his shoes as he entered through the back door.

"Jack almost got caught retrieving the phone," he announced, slapping his gloves down on the heavy oak kitchen table. "He had to ditch it. I put it back, but I doubt he'll get another chance. Obviously Chari doesn't trust him outside alone. By the way, he'll have one less guard to deal with. The guy ran like a rabbit as soon as the other one walked Jack back to the chateau at gunpoint. I sicced the intel guys on him by phone and they picked him up before he got to the road."

Holly and Martine looked up from the layout of the Chari mansion a former employee there had provided. "Can we get someone else inside the house?" Holly asked. "Damn, I wish we could get close enough to listen in on what's happening. At least we have trackers on all their vehicles and their airspace monitored. They can't get the stuff out of there without our knowing."

"Yes, but God only knows what's going on there in the meantime." Eric shook his head as he pulled out one of the chairs and sat down. "I think we're going to have to wing it from here on. I'm not picking up any useful signals from Jack or the doctor today. How about Joe? He get anything?"

"Nothing," Martine told him. "It's a shame these powers of yours and Joe's don't work on command. They're so iffy."

"Most of the time, yeah," Eric said with a sigh. "It's hit or miss. Usually all I need is something belonging to the subject and I get some kind of reading, but Jack's a natural blocker. He's not doing it consciously. It's just his private nature." He ran a hand through his hair and rested his head in his hand. "I wish Will had gone in instead. I can read him like a damn Web page."

Joe and Will walked in. Joe headed straight for the coffeemaker, where he began pouring two cups. "That's because Jack's convinced he doesn't have it. True of most people."

"Like me," Holly admitted. "I *know* I don't. Maybe you both could try Lady Doc again?"

"Already did," Eric said. "All I sense from her is frustration and a truckload of anger. A little fear but not terror. That's a good sign. They've been separated, I do know that."

"How do you know?" Joe asked, sliding into the chair next to Martine. He had been grilling Eric steadily since he had credited that his own flashes of precognition were legitimate on their last case. They were too sporadic and inexplicable to be of any use yet, but he was determined to gain some control.

"How? Well…" The answer was a little embarrassing. Eric hesitated, then forged ahead. No secrets here. "When I did connect with him last evening, Jack was experiencing incredible worry about Solange, as if he couldn't see for himself she was okay. And also he was feeling…you know…sort of physically deprived."

Holly rolled her eyes and groaned. Will sipped his coffee and looked interested. Joe grinned and Martine blushed bright pink.

Then it dawned on Joe, as Eric had known it would, and his grin faded. "Hey, you've never tuned in on anything while we, uh, *they* were…"

"Intimate?" Martine finished the question, her eyes wide with apprehension.

"No, no! Nothing like that," Eric hurried to reassure her. After all, he had been reading her thoughts as well as Joe's like a best-selling adventure novel less than two weeks ago. He'd had to slam those mental books shut a time or two for decency's sake.

"Jack has stepped over the line, messing with a civilian. And on a mission, too," Holly said, clicking her tongue with disbelief. "I'd never have imagined that Mercier, of all people, would—"

"Lighten up, Holly," Joe grumbled. "You're stepping on toes here."

She shrugged. "Hey, man, if the shoe fits. Just because you and Martine got it on and it happened to work out okay, doesn't mean Jack's not gonna get his teeth kicked in when all this is over. He had a rough go of it when his wife got zapped. Since then he's steered way clear of anything serious."

Her sigh echoed what every one of them was thinking. "This sounds serious. He wouldn't have gone this far if it wasn't. But the good doctor has a life here in France. She's not likely to pull up stakes and hook up with a guy who does what we do."

"I did," Martine reminded her.

"Yeah, but your jobs are related and you guys are on the same page. What happens when Jack and Solange get out of there and back to the real world?"

Eric held up his hand to stop this delving into Mercier's love life. "First of all, we need to worry about how we *get* them back to the so-called real world, right?" He looked from one to the other in turn. "Anybody got any bright ideas short of storming the place like a SWAT team?"

Will Griffin spoke up for the first time. "I might have something."

All gazes locked on him. He seldom spoke, but when he did, everybody listened. "The big guy who comes into the village alone and does the purchasing posted some very interesting correspondence for Chari today. Seems our terrorist mogul is now reestablishing his contacts with the world of cinema."

Holly slapped her hands together. "I knew it! See, I

was right." Then she laughed, a dry, mirthless sound. "Something just occurred to me, guys. What if this whole scenario has nothing to do with plaguing the Western world. Not for real, anyway. Could this bio-terror thing be nothing but a hoax? Like he's trying out a film plot or something? Then when somebody finds out and he gets arrested, he gets all sorts of free publicity?"

Will was already shaking his head. "Don't we wish, but no. It's for real, Holly. There's the purchase of all those supplies and lab equipment. The visits to Iran and New York. He's still got to have the money to back this new enterprise he's planning."

He leaned against the counter, calmly drinking his coffee. "And it appears that he had already begun the actual planning. We've agreed that Chari's after making a name for himself in the movies. All signs indicate he's putting out feelers for that. Could mean he expects his money to be available shortly. The toxin might be ready."

"If he's even running the show," Eric said. "Chari could be a dupe for someone else. We've kicked this around before, I know. Anyone have any more ideas while we're s'posing?" He was watching Martine as he spoke. "What are you smiling about, Mrs. Newlywed? You smile entirely too much these days."

"I have an idea." She clasped her hands on the table as if containing her excitement. "We could invite Chari here," she said. "I'm supposed to be the writer with a few screenplays to my credit. What if we offered him film rights he couldn't help but be interested in? You probably couldn't get much information out of him, but if he accepts the invitation, one of you might manage to sneak into the chateau and make contact while he's over here. Or, better yet, if Jack knows he's coming, he might coax Chari into letting him come along as a driver or bodyguard.''

No one said anything as they considered whether it might work. Then Holly, who was heading the backup force for the mission, answered, "Okay, let's give it a shot. Worst he can do is decline."

"There's the local festival happening the day after tomorrow in the village. Could we connect a party to that?" Eric asked.

Holly thought about it. "No. Let's do it the night before. Tomorrow night. Can we get it together by tomorrow night if we hustle?"

Not waiting for an answer, she pointed to Will. "Use whatever contacts you can. As Martine suggested, rustle us up the name of a script that's hot. A best-selling firecracker of a book that Martine, our famous Madame D'Amato, has supposedly just bought film rights to. Story will be that she's looking for a coproducer. It will have to be something that will grab Chari's interest. A potential goldmine."

She pondered a few seconds, then held up a finger. "We need us a few rich and influential guests. Let's make this a real party. Call and see if you can coerce a couple of those guys Chari contacted by mail to fly in."

"I know the *perfect* someone," Eric said, rubbing his hands together in his excitement. "She's in Scotland filming. I bet she'd fly over and bring friends."

Will put down his cup and started for the door that led out back to the garage. "I'll go find a caterer. You're not making me cook for this shindig."

Holly tossed her napkin at him. "With your repertoire? Like we want five-alarm chili? Let's make this a cocktail party. I'm sure you can mix drinks." They all laughed when he looked wounded.

"At least now we can be fairly sure we aren't dealing with a cell of diehards like Al-Qaeda," Martine said with a sigh of relief.

"At least with Chari, we're not, but God only knows who he's selling the stuff to," Eric said. "Or who he might have with him there at the chateau supervising the project. That's what we need to find out."

The moment Jack entered their rooms, he found René pacing, absolutely livid with anger. "Who in *hell* does he think he is?" the boy ranted. "Why is he doing this? She has done nothing! Nothing to him!"

"Shh," Jack warned as René raged loudly against his father for holding Solange in the tower. "Look, I *saw* her today. She is fine! He'll return her to you soon. Now go wash your face and calm down." While he talked, Jack virtually dragged the boy into the bathroom, the only place where they would not be overheard. He twisted the faucet until it ran full force.

"Get her out of there!" René demanded. "You can do it."

"Now you listen to me, kid. This kind of tantrum could get her hurt. Listen to me!" He shook René by the shoulders. The mutinous scowl remained, but the verbal tirade ceased.

"If he doesn't let her go before, I'm going into the tower tomorrow night. You could help by causing a distraction. Can you do that? If I get caught in there, you could share the blame," he warned.

René nodded eagerly. "What shall I do?" Then he answered himself. "I'll run away. The cameras will see me leaving, of course, and the guards will follow, those that are not on the roof. My father might even trouble himself to come out and look for me. He usually doesn't care what I do, but I think he will make an exception this time. If not, you will have to deal with him.''

''That could work. Do it directly after midnight, when the second shift will have gone up. I'll be off duty then and should be summoned to help find and bring you back. Instead of searching, I'll circle around where the roof guards won't see me and try to get up to her window. Those up there are not barred, are they?''

''No, not the ones on the upper floor. And the stones are rough, some of the chinking gone so you can probably scale it. I did it once, coming down, when he shut me up in there.''

''Is there a place you can hide so they won't find you?'' Jack asked.

René nodded. ''The old oak out back. The biggest one. There's a place between the branches where I won't be visible from the ground.''

''I'll come and get you after I've seen Solange and find out what's going on in there. If I bring you back in with me, they will never suspect where I've been.''

Guards always traveled in pairs, told that if one went missing, the other would pay for it with his life. Jack wondered why Piers had not been even more upset when Edouard had deserted. Piers seemed exempt from the usual rules.

Chari would send Jack with someone, of course. He just hoped it wouldn't be Piers. Any of the others he could put out of commission temporarily with no trouble at all.

René frowned. ''I'll watch for you to come down from the tower and meet you at the foot. But you will bring Dr. Micheaux out with you? You will send her somewhere safe?''

Jack shook his head. ''No, René. If she is being well treated, she must stay there until I can convince your father to let her go, but I want to question her and make certain she is as well as she seemed today. We must not play our hand too soon. Many lives may depend on how we deal with this. Do you understand?''

The boy agreed, reluctantly. Jack hoped he could trust him.

For the rest of the afternoon, the off-duty guards like Jack cleaned all of the weapons, played cards or watched movies. Chari had a vast collection from which to choose. It was what they did every day, a monotonous routine.

Jack took one of the DVD players and several movies in to René to keep him occupied. And also to check whether boredom had fostered any wilder plan than the one they had hatched together for the following night.

There were no more sightings of movement in the trees as Jack stood watch that night. No more quarrels with messages attached shot onto the roof.

He tried again to send a mental message, hoping either Eric or Joe would receive it. Eyes closed, he attempted to focus his mind and project clear thoughts. *Hold off. We are okay. Not enough info yet.*

Before this mission, he had never really tried to communicate by thought, but this seemed the most logical and straightforward method to do it. Like a one-way phone call. Thought mail. And amazingly it seemed to have worked.

At the moment, though, he realized his mind was probably too cluttered for it to actually work. He couldn't seem to clear his head of extraneous thoughts. Like the constant imagining of predicaments Solange could be encountering.

The next morning Solange noted that Belclair seemed less driven than usual. He took his time setting everything up, even hummed a little as he plodded through his routine. As usual he ignored her unless he wanted her to save him a few steps.

He had not asked her to record yesterday's tests or the findings. At precisely ten o'clock, he excused himself and waddled out. His knocking on the door upstairs echoed down to the lab where he had left the door standing open.

This was not good, she thought. This must mean he had made some sort of breakthrough.

She crept closer to the doorway and listened until she heard the sound of voices and the door close again. He did not return, so she supposed he had gone into the study with Chari. Quickly she rushed up to his room to see if she could find the log there. But the door was securely locked.

When she started to turn away, she heard voices within. But he had gone upstairs! Who was in there? She listened more closely and realized what it was. This room was where the receivers were for the microphones placed in other parts of the chateau! Belclair was the one monitoring everyone else, not Chari himself.

When Belclair did not return, Solange remained in the lab alone. She stared at the storage room where the containers of the substance lay incubating, a womb hatching death.

Solange fiddled with the thermostat, but it seemed locked at the temperature he had set for it, and nothing she did lowered it by so much as a degree. She kept working on it, her ears tuned for Belclair's return.

He never came back.

When Piers arrived in the lab around noon, he brought no tray of food, only a summons. "You are to come with me."

"Now?" she asked.

Piers nodded. Solange gave the lab one last baleful glance and followed him out.

When she arrived upstairs, Chari was standing, obviously waiting. He said nothing until Piers had gone out and closed the door. Then he addressed her rather sharply. "Mercier assures me you can be trusted. If he is wrong, he will answer for it. So will you. Are we understood?"

Solange took a deep breath. Was he about to reveal secrets to her? She could hardly credit he would do that, given his obvious dislike of her. "I will do whatever he says I should do. You are the man who can give us what we want," she answered.

"But you do understand the ramifications if you so much as hint at my doing research of any kind here."

"Yes, I understand." Solange fought for patience. He spoke to her as if she were a simple-minded fool.

He started out the door without another word, curtly beckoning her to follow. She glanced up at the cameras stationed in the corridor as they passed them.

Where was he taking her? Jacques was nowhere to be seen. Where was he? Did he know Chari was taking her somewhere?

They climbed the main staircase and he led her to a room at the very end. When they entered, she saw it was a chamber outfitted for a woman, done in pastel blue with accents of white. It was a lovely place, though old-fashioned. The furniture covered with a fine layer of dust. Did he intend for her to stay here now? And if so, why?

She said nothing as she watched him cross the room and open another door. "Find something in here that will be suitable for an evening out."

"What?" she asked, dumbfounded.

"You are to accompany me this evening. Do you speak English?"

She nodded and shrugged, wondering whether she should risk lying. "A little."

"Well, you will not do so this evening. Is that understood? In fact, I wish you to speak as little as possible in any language to anyone. You will not be allowed to leave my side, even to relieve yourself, so take care of that before we leave. We should be away no more than two or three hours."

"Why are you taking *me?*" she asked.

"That is none of your business. You will come and you will follow orders. If you cannot do that, I will no longer have need of you," he stated. "Or Mercier, for that matter. You know what that means."

"Yes," she said, looking inside the room where hung a woman's wardrobe. Dresses on satin-padded hangers lined one side of the small dressing room. Shelves along the opposite wall contained shoes, purses and assorted accessories.

She went in past him and began to examine more closely what was there. Everything looked woefully dated, the styles at least a decade old. Not that she cared much for fashion, but the clothes also looked a few sizes too large for her and probably had belonged to a much older woman. "I am sorry, these will not fit me," she told him.

"There's a sewing machine in the maid's quarters, through there." He pointed at the door leading out the other side of the dressing room. "Make one fit," he ordered. "That blue silk should do," he said, pointing. "Be ready in two hours."

"I have no makeup or even a hairbrush," she complained. "There is a comb in the room where I stayed before. May I go and get it?"

She fluffed her tousled hair to show its sad state of repair. For three days now she had been letting it dry naturally, combing and scrunching it into waves with her fingers. Maybe he would allow her to go back to the room she had shared with René and dress there, possibly giving her a chance to find Jacques and see if he knew what this was all about.

"There are those things you will need at the dressing table in the bedroom. Piers will come for you later."

As he turned to leave, Solange asked, "Whose room is this?"

"René's grandmother's," he said curtly, surprising her that he had answered at all. He left then, locking the door behind him.

An hour later, Solange had done the best she could with what she had. The gown looked all right, she supposed, which was fortunate since any sewing machine would have baffled her. There had been no one to teach her to sew when she was a girl and she'd had no real inclination to learn.

The cosmetics she found proved stale. She opted for a bit of the powder, a very light touch of the brow pencil to darken her eyebrows and lashes. The lipstick was too old to use, but she fashioned a gloss from the lip pencil color and a dot of the petroleum jelly that had survived the years.

She brushed her hair to a high shine and caught it up with a rhinestone clip she discovered while searching the drawers.

The full-length mirror promised she would not win any trophies for haute couture. However, she had to admit this was a nice change from the wrinkled clothing she had worn and washed repeatedly since coming here.

It appeared Chari was in need of a date for some event. But was it local? She hoped so. Given that Jacques's compatriots were living in Tournade, awaiting the information she and Jacques were here to obtain, it could be that she might see one of them. Surely they were keeping watch on the chateau to monitor who arrived and left. Wouldn't they go to any lengths to make contact with her?

But she would not dare speak to them if that happened, so how could she possibly pass on what she and Jacques had discovered so far?

She went back into the dressing room and located a small, beaded evening bag. A thrill of excitement buoyed her hopes. In the purse she found a lace-edged linen handkerchief.

With the eye pencil, she scribbled on the fabric the formula that Belclair had last entered in his log book. That might have changed yesterday, but if she found a chance to pass it on to them, at least they would have some idea of what the threat was.

She felt like Mata Hari. Would Jacques approve of her taking this chance? It could mean both their lives if Chari found the handkerchief or caught her passing it on to those people, if the opportunity arose.

What else could she tell the agents? Solange pondered for a few minutes. She wrote the word *used* and added a question mark. She had found no reference to any of the substance being sent anywhere, but neither was there any proof that it had not.

What more had she found out? Frustrated by the lack of her success as a spy, Solange sought desperately for something else to impart. The chemist's name might be of help. At least they would know who was doing the actual research and that he was working alone. She wrote his name and added the word *only*.

Hopefully they could decipher what she was giving them. If not, they would at least know that she was trying.

Ready as she was going to get for a night out with a local terrorist leader, Solange folded the handkerchief so that the writing was concealed. Then she tucked it, the eye and lip pencils and a comb inside the bag.

Chapter 10

When Piers came for her, Solange had heard him coming up and was sitting in the damask wing chair thumbing through a photo album she'd found. She put it aside immediately and picked up the little purse.

"I will take that," he said and did so, rudely snatching it out of her hand.

Solange held her breath as he snapped it open and poked two fingers inside it, feeling around, she supposed for anything sharp. After only a cursory glance at the contents, he handed it back to her. "Come with me," he ordered.

She hid her relief. So far, so good.

Solange accompanied Piers down the main staircase to the foyer. Chari and Jacques were both there. For a moment she hoped Jacques was being allowed to chauffeur, but Chari relieved her of that notion when he ordered Piers to bring the car.

"A shame that a limousine is out of the question,"

Chari said to no one in particular, flicking imaginary lint from the lapels of his tuxedo.

Solange fastened her gaze on Jacques who was looking rather stunned, she guessed, by her appearance. It was totally at odds with the only conditions he had seen her in thus far. She offered him a wry smile.

His eyes grew hard, erasing the brief glimpse of surprise and pleasure she had seen in them. "Are you not afraid of compromising your security by attending this little soiree?" he asked, addressing Chari. "The guests there could have friends in high places. Sophia D'Amato, inaccessible as she has been to the public, has written books with political themes. She might have connections who would be extremely interested in preventing what you are doing," he said.

"Her 'connections' are precisely what I am wanting to use." Chari smiled slyly. "The project here has nothing at all to do with my business tonight. Except for providing funds, of course. As for the security aspect, we need not worry. Not at all," Chari replied evenly. His heavy-lidded gaze fell on her.

"Why are you taking Solange?" Jacques asked, a note of jealousy tinging the question. She knew it was deliberate. A little reverse psychology, she supposed. She was no psychologist, but anyone could see that Chari was a prime subject for it.

Chari continued to study her for a moment, then shrugged. "I could hardly attend an affair such as this alone, and she *is* the only woman available to go with me. She knows what will happen if she talks out of turn. Don't you, Doctor?"

Solange nodded, all compliance. Jacques had mentioned the writer D'Amato, Martine Corda's assumed identity. Was the affair to be at the very place Jacques had taken her before coming here? This was better than she could have hoped. She wanted nothing to prevent her going. She had a handkerchief to drop.

Anticipation fostered a genuine smile, and she turned it on Jacques, hoping to reassure him that she was taking care of the matter. "Do not fret, Jacques," she told him. "I promise I shall be the perfect escort for Monsieur Chari tonight." She clutched the small beaded purse to her chest and gave it a small pat as she looked up at her date. "Shall we go?"

Jacques opened the front door for them, managing to look both disgruntled and resigned, drawing a chuckle from Chari as he led Solange outside. She risked a peek out the window and a small wave as they drove away. He stood in the doorway watching. He was wearing his spy face, she noted, the one that held no expression whatsoever, the one he never wore when they were together alone. She must thank him for that because it chilled her to the bone.

Solange turned her attention to Chari, who seemed restless, perhaps even nervous.

"I read one of Madame D'Amato's books several years ago," Solange said just to break the silence. "I believe it was called *Dark Menace*. Have you read her?"

"Not that one," Chari snapped. "You may tell her you have read it. Be effusive when you do. Say you enjoyed it," he ordered.

"Actually, I did." The real author was legend, but extremely reclusive. Solange wondered if the woman had actually agreed to tonight's impersonization. Perhaps she had and would one day use the situation in one of her novels or screenplays.

"Do something with your hair," he demanded. "You

look disheveled and unkempt. Everyone will pity me, bringing someone who looks like you.''

Solange shrugged and tucked a stray curl behind her ear, then brushed another back away from her face. She bit off the sharp retort that popped to mind. It was not worth making him angry. He might have Piers turn the car around, take her back and go alone. She hung her head and slumped her shoulders, an attitude he seemed to like in a woman.

His words reminded her too much of the last weeks she had spent with Jean. That beating down of her self-worth, the cruel verbal jabs at her looks and intelligence. She could hardly wait until this man got his just desserts. And she was damned glad she would have a hand in it.

She watched the passing scenery without displaying much interest. It was nearly dark, but she noted every landmark they passed, every turn, every feature of the landscape. She timed the trip on the auto's clock as Piers drove. Twenty minutes from door to door.

The small mansion appeared quite different bathed in light. Outdoor spots highlighted the ornate stonework of the facade and the heavily carved and arched double doors. Huge pots of geraniums and greenery flanked the portal and steps leading in. Quite a transition from intimidating to charming in a matter of days.

They were met by the same man who had greeted her and Jacques before. He was tall, well built and quite handsome in a dark red dinner jacket. One of madame's staff tonight, Solange thought with a smile. He opened the door on her side of the car and offered her a hand. She accepted his assistance and got out. Chari quickly followed, taking a firm hold on her arm. The man gave

Piers instructions for parking, then ushered her and Chari inside.

Holly Amberson, striking in ecru and pearls, greeted them in heavily accented French and guided them into the huge salon. "I am Kerry, Madame D'Amato's personal assistant. You must be M'sieu Ahmed Chari! Madame was delighted to hear that you were in residence nearby and simply had to have you here." She looked questioningly at Solange.

Solange introduced herself, since Chari did not. "I am Solange. So nice to meet you."

"Just Solange?" Holly asked with an interested smile.

"Yes." With a small inclination of her head, she ended the exchange. Holly gave a neat little shrug that said she couldn't care less and turned full attention back to Chari.

He, busy scanning the room for familiar faces, assured Holly that he was quite proficient in English if she wished to switch languages so that he could understand her. He could not abide American accents.

His blatant insult did nothing to dampen Holly's enthusiasm.

She sighed with obvious relief. "Oh, that's wonderful! There are several guests present who will appreciate that. Madame will be down soon. May I introduce you to some of the others?" She snaked one arm through the crook of Chari's and fairly dragged him across the salon. Since Chari's fingers were still biting into her arm, Solange followed.

"Here is Bev Martin, who needs no introduction. Ms. Martin, meet Ahmed Chari, Tournade's most famous resident, though only the locals know he is here! And his friend, Solange, of course."

"Of course." The tall, gorgeous brunette gave Chari the once-over, her dark lashes sweeping up and down. She paused to sip the martini she held, then cleared her throat. "I do believe we met in Cannes several years ago."

Chari had taken the actress's hand and raised it almost to his lips. "You were magnificent in *Siege of Malabar*. I have seen it many times since. Such nuances in your performance. One must view it repeatedly to catch them all."

"High praise indeed," she said in the silky voice that had made her famous. "Thank you, Ahmed. Tell me, have you anything in progress now?"

Solange was certain she could have slipped away right then and Chari would never notice she was gone. But if he should, she was not ready to face the consequences. She stayed where she was to see what would happen next. She felt certain that was what Jacques would have her do.

Holly nudged Solange's elbow, got her attention then looked pointedly at the man standing next to Bev Martin. "This rascal is Eric Vinland. He keeps us all smiling, especially Bev. Watch out for him." She punched him playfully on the arm with her impossibly long, pearl-colored fingernail and left them to mingle.

The man called Eric smiled directly at her and lifted his glass in a salute. She remembered hearing Jacques ask about an Eric's whereabouts the night they had stopped here.

"Hi, Solange. You shouldn't mind Holly. She likes to tease her old friends," he said as if he had read her thoughts. He pointed at Chari and the actress with his drink. "Would you like to go to the bar with me while these two talk shop? That fellow they've hired makes a mean martini.''

This was it! He was the one. He was making contact with her.

Chari's hand tightened on her arm. She glanced down at it. "Uh, no thank you." She pasted on a wide smile. "Maybe later."

He nodded knowingly and moved away from the little group toward the bar set up on the other side of the salon. Solange's heart skipped with panic. Holly was nowhere to be seen, now the one called Eric had deserted her, too.

Chari was oozing charm all over the gorgeous actress, intimating that he would love to work with her one day if she were available. He was sugarcoating his vague offer with lavish compliments that made Solange want to gag. Couldn't the poor woman see how false he was? How evil?

However, the woman was eating the praise with a spoon. It amazed Solange that anyone would be nice to this man. True, he was handsome enough. It was just when he opened his mouth and spoke, one got the full effect of Chari.

She glared at his back. Pretentious, chauvinistic pig that he was, she would love to take a cleaver and make him into pork chops.

A burst of laughter at the bar caught her attention. The man named Eric was propped there, looking at her. He winked and laughed again. She smiled back, simply because she was so happy to see a friendly face.

God, she wished Jacques were here. What would he do? How would he get the message to his people?

She opened her purse and took out the folded handkerchief. The next time one of them came near her, she would drop it. They would surely be watching for something like that. Wouldn't they?

She looked again toward the bar. The handsome Eric nodded, toasted her with his drink and turned away.

In addition to the actress, she and Chari met several other people in the film world whom Solange knew by name. Pierre Trident, an award-winning director, spoke quite fervently about Chari's last film. How had they managed this guest list? Solange wondered.

And there was Guy Marque, the tall, dark and moody actor who had won last year's Oscar at the American awards ceremony. His personal antics around the world made the news quite regularly. He looked much smaller in person. It was a stellar gathering, and Chari seemed nervous and eager. Trying too hard to fit in.

The pianist who had been playing softly in the background suddenly struck several loud chords to get attention. Conversation ceased. In the doorway of the salon stood a gorgeous older woman, a vision in lace and chiffon. Her silvery hair was styled to perfection.

"Good evening, everyone!" she said, waving one hand. "I apologize for arriving late to my own party, but it takes longer these days to create the mask."

She laughed along with her guests and motioned for the music to resume. As it did she made her way from group to group, accepting accolades on her latest publication and offering teasing comments to each person.

Solange watched her and realized Chari was doing the same. "She looks nothing like I thought she would," Solange said. "I expected her to be much younger."

"What would you know?" he growled.

"You can release my arm," she told him. "People will think you are too possessive. I promise I am not going anywhere. Besides, you will need both hands for the buffet.''

She tried very hard to sound merely practical and not sarcastic. It would not do to anger him. He might decide to leave before she had a chance to speak to anyone else.

To her surprise he let go of her, but pinned her with a look of warning that said she had better stay close. He saw to it that she did.

The rest of the evening flew by for Solange as she watched desperately for a chance to pass her information to either Holly or Eric. She carried the handkerchief in her hand, waiting. Neither came anywhere near her.

Sophia D'Amato beckoned Chari to join her on the damask divan. He almost tripped over Solange in his hurry to respond. He took his seat next to the author, and Solange sat on his other side, as ordered.

The woman wasted no time. ''I have purchased the film rights to *Descent of Fools*.''

''By Sim Gordoni? My, what an undertaking!'' Chari exclaimed, his dark eyes rounding with awe. ''Will you do the screenplay yourself?''

''With Gordoni's input, yes.''

''But this is so exciting!'' Chari gushed. ''It is certain to win acclaim on all fronts!''

She accepted the idea with a confident nod. ''We will need a coproducer. Do you know anyone who might be interested?'' She quirked one sharply arched eyebrow, but it seemed to be an effort for her.

The woman wore such thick makeup, she looked as if she dared not smile, but her eyes were surprisingly clear. Blue as a lagoon with the sun shining through it.

Chari almost gasped the word, ''Yes! I would be

most interested myself! This would be a great honor for me, Madame D'Amato. I cannot tell you how—''

"Yes, yes. Good enough. We will talk particulars later,'' she said, pushing her slender body up from the divan. She looked down at him. "I shall have my people call you. Now if you will excuse me, please.''

Without waiting for an answer, she walked away, shuffling as if her hips ached. That cane she carried was not an affectation as Solange had thought when she'd first seen it.

Perhaps she could use a prescription for something to alleviate her pain. Solange had expected the agent portraying D'Amato to be a much younger woman. Though she had not met Martine Corda, Jacques and Holly had spoken of her assuming this role. The woman was recently wed to one of the agents, Joseph Corda, they had said. And yet, Solange saw no older man who might be the husband.

The bartender seemed too adept at his job to be one of them. He handled the bottles and glasses as if born to do what he was doing instead of being an undercover agent. The mysterious one called Will who had met them at the car that night was nowhere to be seen.

She gave up trying to figure all of that out and returned to looking for an opportunity to deliver her message without being caught.

At last, just as they were leaving, Eric joined them at the door, ostensibly waiting for his driver to pull his car around as soon as theirs arrived and departed.

"Mr. Chari, Solange, great to meet you. You know, I almost missed coming tonight? My father had a small accident and is in hospital, but he was doing so incredibly well, I decided to come after all.''

"Oh, I'm *so* glad,'' Solange said fervently.

She knew, just knew, he was imparting a message to her about her own father. He was well. Incredibly well. She laughed softly and shrugged.

Chari shifted impatiently, not bothering to speak to someone he would consider an underling, maybe even a plaything for the great actress, Bev Martin. "Here is our driver now," he snapped.

Solange smiled at Eric, feeling enormous relief that he had presented himself before it was too late.

"It was nice meeting you, too, Eric," she said with heartfelt honesty. With her hand at her side, concealed by the folds of her dress, she dropped the handkerchief at his feet and turned away.

She sensed him crouch behind her as she followed Chari through the open door.

"Oh, Solange! Wait a minute!"

Chari turned with her and glared at Eric. "Yes, what is it?" he asked.

"The lady lost her hanky," Eric said, holding it out to her. "Too pretty to lose," he said with a grin.

Chari grabbed it from Eric, hustled her out the door and into the waiting car.

Solange's heart sank to her knees. All was lost.

Chapter 11

"Stupid cow!" Chari shouted. As soon as they were well away from the house, he switched on the dome light, fumbling and cursing as he did so.

Solange closed her eyes and waited for the death threats. Or possibly the reality of death itself.

He need not wait until they were back at the chateau to strangle her. And he would. Chari's violent nature shone from his eyes like the evil light that it was. Jacques would suffer for this, too. She had failed miserably.

"Trying to seduce Bev Martin's lover? What were you thinking? You women are all the same!" he shouted.

Seduce? He was shouting at her for flirting!

Solange risked looking over at him. Oh, God, he was examining the handkerchief. Any minute now he would see the writing...

Suddenly he flung the scrap of lace and fabric at her

face and slammed himself angrily back against the car seat. "You could have cost me my star!"

Solange wondered if she could even speak. Quickly she stuffed the handkerchief back into the beaded purse and heaved out a breath of relief. He had not seen the writing on it. How had he not seen that? Even if it had smudged to illegibility, he would have questioned it. She clenched her eyes shut and offered up a prayer of thanks.

Chari had already forgotten the handkerchief. "She will agree to work with me. I know she will," he muttered. "She looked at me with respect. That one liked what she saw in Cannes! For a woman, she has re-markable taste. Except for that *boy* she keeps."

He cursed foully and slammed a fist in his palm. "You with your sluttish attempt to seduce him could have spoiled everything, do you hear? *Everything,* damn you!"

He ranted all the way back to the chateau. By the time they arrived, her tower prison was almost looking good to her. Anything to get away from this head case.

It made her sick to think of the verbal abuse René and his poor mother must have suffered during their years with this man.

The minute the car stopped, she climbed out and reached the house first. Piers was ahead of both of them and opened the door.

Chari shoved her inside, straight into Jacques's arms. For the few seconds allowed, she gave in to her need, crowded close to his body and absorbed some of his strength. He held her, saying nothing.

"Take the bitch to your room since she is in heat!" Chari thundered as he stormed inside, pointing down the hallway. "See that she stays there. I do not wish to see her again."

Before Jacques could follow his order, Chari halted him. "Wait! It is not even ten o'clock. Why are you not standing guard?"

"I exchanged shifts with Victor. Your son was not feeling well this evening, and I thought someone should stay with him."

Then Jacques headed quickly in the direction of their rooms, keeping her in front of him. She managed to hold back her tears until they reached the room where René was waiting.

The second the door closed, she broke down. Furious with herself, with Chari and the world, she tried to stop, but the tears only came faster. She beat her fists against the nearest solid object, which happened to be Jacques's chest. He held her loosely and absorbed the blows until she tired.

When she finally regained control, René was there, offering her a wet hand towel.

She smiled grimly as she accepted it and began to wash her face. "I am sorry," she whispered. "This is not like me. Not at all."

The boy brushed a hand along her arm and gave her a pat of comfort. Jacques drew her more firmly against him until she pushed away. She looked up at him and repeated, "I *am* sorry, Jacques. I tried to—"

He raised a finger to her lips to warn her not to say anything. She had been about to do just that. Too long in that tower, she had forgotten about the hidden microphones in this room.

René, questioning with his eyes, jerked his thumb toward the bathroom as he backed toward it. She and Jacques followed.

"What happened?" René whispered, his dark eyes wide with worry.

Solange sighed as she leaned back against the sink and raised the purse to open it and show them what she had attempted to do.

She pulled out the lacy handkerchief. Only it was not the handkerchief at all. It appeared to be a square of someone's lingerie. Lace ran along two sides of it and the other two were simply sheared off.

She began to laugh, clutching the scrap of fabric to her. "He saw it in my hand. He knew," she cried. "Somehow he knew what it was. Your Eric *knew*."

Jacques and René looked at each other in confusion.

"She is not well," René declared. "I think you should give her one of those pills she brought for me and put her straight to bed."

Solange laughed even harder, shaking her head as Jacques clasped an arm around her shoulders and guided her into his bedroom. He touched a finger to her lips again to signal her the microphone was active again.

René followed, hovering close, obviously unsure what to do with a hysterical female who had lost her senses. She made an effort to appear sane, but she wasn't certain she really was at the moment. She leaned on Jacques until he placed her gently on the bed. He inclined his head, a silent order for René to leave them alone.

Solange reached out quickly and grasped René's hand. "Thank you for caring, René," she said to him and smiled. "It is simply the relief of having the evening over. I was very nervous, but now I will be fine. How are you?"

He shrugged uncertainly. "Good." Then he cast another glance at Jacques and backed out of the room.

"Here, lie down," Jacques said to her. "Go to sleep. Tomorrow is time enough to talk. I cannot believe you angered him on purpose," he scolded, his voice a bit too loud. Solange knew it was for the benefit of anyone listening through the microphone.

"I did nothing but act pleasantly to people!" she argued, sniffling for effect. "He thought I was making a bid for some actress's lover! I would never, never betray you in such a way. You have to believe me."

"Why should I?" he grumbled.

"Jacques, please do not be angry. All I did was smile. I accidentally dropped something, and the man picked it up for me. Chari thought I did it on purpose to get attention, but it was not intentional. That was all that happened, I promise."

"Go to sleep. I do not want to hear it!" he almost shouted the words.

All the while he was busy disconnecting the microphone in the base of the lamp. As soon as he had done that, he took her in his arms again. "Now tell me. What have you done?"

"I wrote everything I knew about the project on a handkerchief. I thought perhaps your people would follow if we left the chateau and try to make contact if they could. If nothing else, they would want to know how you were faring."

"Solange!"

She ignored his protest. It was done, right or wrong, and nothing she could do now would change that. "To my surprise, we went right into their midst, to the house in Tournade. Chari kept me close. I had no chance to speak with them about anything here. But the man called Eric was there. He saw the handkerchief and must have guessed it might be important. When he picked it up for me, he had another ready, a quickly found substitute, but it served the purpose.''

"Thank God.''

She laughed again, a tinny sound, high pitched and bordering on hysteria. ''One of your friends has a piece of her slip missing, I believe.'' She took a deep breath and tried to regain her equilibrium. Her nerves were still jangling like sleigh bells.

Jacques pressed his fingertips on the bridge of his nose and shook his head. He blew out his breath slowly as if trying to marshal his emotions. Then he spoke clearly, concisely and with a firmness she had not witnessed since he took her from the prison by force. ''You will never, never try anything so risky again, Solange. Give me your word.''

She nodded eagerly, then slipped her arms around him. ''Oh, Jacques, I have missed you so.''

He groaned as he found her lips with his and kissed her breath away. No further words passed between them as he slipped the loose-fitting silk dress over her head and covered her skin with kisses. He touched her everywhere, pausing only to unsnap her bra and slide the rest of her clothing away.

As eager as he, Solange unbuttoned his trousers and slid down the zipper. He pushed his clothing down past his hips and fit their bodies together as if speed were critical.

She sighed as he sank deep within her, imbuing her with his strength and driving every thought from her mind but the pleasure of having him.

He moved slowly, the effort drawing gasps from him and pleas from her as they loved. Solange welcomed the glorious tension that built with each thrust, forcing the fear and worry out of her like magic.

He silenced her cry of completion with his mouth, a kiss that rivaled the act of love itself.

When he tensed and gave a final thrust, she watched his face, loved the way he gave of everything he was in that instant when time stood still for them.

If only they could hold this moment forever, she thought sadly. If only she could hold *him*.

It was not to be, but the wish was there, and she stopped denying it to herself. If he would have her, she would have him, no matter who he was or what he did or why.

She realized that she loved Jacques Mercier. And she was not even certain that was really his name.

A tear leaked out of her eye and she felt it trail slowly down her cheek, a hot reminder of where they were and what they were supposed to be doing.

His sigh was long and heartfelt as he lay beside her, his fingers idly toying with her hair. He drew the clasp free slowly, carefully and tossed it away.

"You looked so beautiful tonight," he said. "When I saw you come down those stairs, I wanted to grab you and run, take you away from all of this and let the devil take these bastards. Solange, I have to end it."

"Us?" she asked.

"No, them," he answered.

"I think the research has drawn to a close," she informed him. "The one chemist Chari has working in the lab must have succeeded in what he was trying to do."

"What was that?" The languor had left his voice and he was all business, the dedicated agent. No longer the lover.

"Making the toxin stable regardless of temperature," she told him, condensing the research she had been privy to as concisely as she could for a layman's ear.

Then she repeated what she had written down on the handkerchief.

"The formula is the last one that he recorded, but I believe he made some sort of breakthrough after that entry. The log disappeared and I couldn't find it."

"My God, don't tell me you were plundering through his things looking for it. You could have been caught!"

She shook her head impatiently. "I was safe enough. After he came to whatever conclusion he reached, he left. Apparently he had a key all along and could come and go as he pleased. I was locked in the tower alone until Chari came for me and took me upstairs to get ready for tonight."

"I have to move on this right away," Jacques said, sitting up and running a hand through his hair. "God knows, I'm ready to get out of here and I *know* you must be."

"What do we do?" Solange asked, placing her palm on his back, feeling the hard muscles play beneath her hand. "How may I help?"

He looked down at her and smiled. "Don't you think you've done enough?" His smile was grim. "Are you sure you're not with Sécurité or something like it?"

"I do not even know the names of our agencies. No, I am simply a doctor who, until this past week, was as unaware of imminent threats such as this as the next person."

"And now here you are, up to your beautiful neck in *very* imminent threats."

She caressed his back, gently scraping her nails along

the ridge of his spine. "Yes. And here you are, burdened with a bumbling novitiate."

"No longer that." He smiled and reclined, trapping her arm beneath him, sliding his palm over her midsection and touching her intimately. "I hate that it was I who stole your innocence."

"I was hardly innocent," she argued lazily, her mind already dismissing everything but the feel of his hand on her.

"Oh, yes, Solange, you were. But tonight we will forget where we are, all that has happened and all that is to come. We have our time out of time."

"Yes," she whispered, "at least we have that."

Jack left Solange sleeping when he went to pull the late shift that would last until dawn. René had promised to keep watch over her and raise the roof if anyone came to order her back to the tower.

It was doubtful Chari would do that, at least not tonight. He had said he did not want to see her again. Best case, he would want her to remain in their rooms until he was ready to get rid of her. And if what Solange suspected were true, that the toxin was ready for distribution, the time was near.

Chari would want everyone disposed of, all loose ends neatly tied up. Jack just hoped he was the one appointed executioner when the time came. At least he would have a weapon in his hands. He hefted the one he held now and thought about going ahead with the task and including Chari in the sweep.

He had a strong feeling it would be foolish to risk waiting any longer for information he might never get. His gut was telling him to move and move soon. But he couldn't do it at the end of his shift. He needed a little time to prepare Solange and René for the show-down so they wouldn't get in his way and get hurt.

That would mean operating with no weapon, taking them out one at the time. Not a problem if he could somehow get around the cameras and maintain the element of surprise. The guards were not issued weapons unless they were on duty. The weapons room was kept locked until change of shift, and Piers kept the key. Of all the guards, only he carried one all the time.

Help would be good. Jack only hoped Eric was awake and alert. He focused his whole mind in the direction of Tournade.

Noon. Be here at noon. Arrive in force. Jack thought the words repeatedly until other thoughts, other worries intruded. It was damned difficult to keep everything else blanked out even for the few seconds it took. All the channels of his mind were surely scrambling one another.

He took a deep breath, tried a little meditation, then went at it again, knowing he was trying too hard, that it was highly unlikely that even a truly gifted psychic could make any sense of it. *Get the word* noon, *if nothing else!* he projected with a final blast of thought.

Damn. This was useless. Here he was with an automatic in his hands, trying to summon backup with his mind. It went against all his training and seemed patently ridiculous. He should go down those stairs, blow away the bad guys and let the chips fall where they may. But it was too soon for that.

There had to be someone else, someone with more brains than Chari, inside the chateau directing this drama, someone with an unknown agenda. Suppose that man was the one freak in this sideshow willing to die for his cause. Then what?

One final attempt should be made to discover the identity of the one in charge. Jack decided if he had not done that by noon, he would wind this up, anyway.

When the sun came up and his shift was over, Jack reluctantly handed over his weapon and handset to his replacement and went back to his room. It was almost time for breakfast and he needed to speak with Solange and René to get them ready for what was going down in a few hours.

The instant he entered he knew something was wrong. René was not in his room and neither was Solange. They were not in the other bedroom, either, and the door to the bathroom was closed. Water was running.

He rattled the doorknob. "Solange?"

Locked, but he heard the immediate snick of the key as it turned. Her hand snaked out and grabbed his arm, pulling him inside. She closed the door, almost slammed it behind him and stood against it, pointing to René and the instrument he was holding to his ear. "What? What is that?"

"An infant monitor," she whispered. "René managed to plant the other part in Chari's study after you went on guard. He remembered the thing being in the box with his old toys and we thought it was worth trying. He took the batteries out of—"

René put a finger to his lips and handed the receiver over to Jack. "Listen!"

Jack grabbed it. The voice sounded scratchy, but readily identifiable. Piers was speaking.

"...see how effective it is before they implement it abroad. The festival today is perfect."

"No. The formula is viable now, I tell you! We need no further tests. Three have succumbed to it with minimal contact. I say we proceed as planned," argued another voice, definitely French. A native, but not Chari. Here was the unknown quantity.

Then Chari did enter into the mix. "I agree with Brus. Not in Tournade. That would be madness, Piers! Who do you think will be the primary suspect if we test it there? Who is the one resident of this area of Iranian descent, eh? Do not be an imbecile!"

A loud smack and a cry of pain ensued.

"Tournade," Piers declared. "Go and get it for me now. I will leave here at nine. The crowd will be gathering by that time for the day's activities. We will spread it for maximum contact and be out of there in less than half an hour. Both of you pack up and be ready to move out by the time I return."

"Leave?" Chari demanded. "I cannot leave here now!"

"You will. In the twenty-four hours before the symptoms appear, we can each depart separately and reunite in Greece as planned. When news of the attack is announced, our buyer will have his verification and bring us the balance payment."

"This is a waste of time," the stranger said, but it was a quiet objection, not strident as before.

When Solange's hand tugged at his arm, Jack shot her a questioning look.

"That is Belclair," she whispered, "the chemist."

So this was a triumvirate, Jack thought, with Piers at the head. What was his agenda? Money, of course, but it seemed to Jack that if the toxin was ready, as the chemist had confirmed, this little test run was indeed an unnecessary risk for them to take.

Three had succumbed. That would have been the two

agents sent in undercover by French intelligence and perhaps the lab assistant whom Solange had replaced.

If they proceeded with this test at the local festival, the trail would inevitably lead to Chari. The world knew his face because of his notoriety with the films. When taken into custody and questioned, he could expose them all. Either Piers did not care or he intended to eliminate the weak link before anything really hit the fan.

The voices had gone silent. A door slammed. Jack gripped René's shoulder. "Is there anywhere you and Solange can conceal yourselves inside the chateau until I wrap this up?"

René was already shaking his head. "Not without the camera picking us up as we go. When I planted the monitor, I didn't even try to avoid being seen. I simply marched into the study, plunked down in a chair and demanded a moment of my father's time. He ordered me back to my room, but not before I slipped the monitor under the chair." He grinned. "That was brilliant, was it not?"

Jack rolled his eyes and sighed. "Brilliant, but highly risky." He had to admit it was a stroke of genius, though he might never have agreed to the plan if he had been consulted.

He would have to work fast. It was nearly eight o'clock now. Piers would be leaving for Tournade with the toxin at nine.

It was highly likely that Martine and Joe would be attending that festival. Will would almost surely be there to see whether Chari or Piers would turn up at the postal facility or the grocers. They would be as much at risk as the rest of the population if the ricin vaccine didn't protect against the new substance.

Stopping Piers was the first order of business. He grabbed Solange's hand. "Can you drive?"

She nodded briskly. "Anything with wheels."

"Good. You'll come with me. René? You are to create a distraction. Any kind, the bigger the better. Draw as much attention here as you possibly can. See if you can do something to set off the smoke alarms. That should bring the guards off the roof."

"Now?"

"Right now," Jack agreed. Then he turned to Solange. "You be ready to run. We are heading for the kitchen. The keys to the vehicles are kept in a locked cabinet. I'll break it open and give them all to you."

"All? Oh, so they can't follow?"

He nodded. "At least it will slow them down. I'll disable the two guarding the back entrance. You run to the garage, take whatever wheels are nearest the entrance, find the keys that fit and drive straight to the house in Tournade. Warn the team what Piers plans so they can intercept him outside the village. And have them call in some backup for me. Got it?"

"Got it! I will hurry!" she replied. "Jacques, please—"

"Be careful, I know. Same goes," he ordered with a quick brush of his hand over her shoulder. "Remember, I love you."

Her eyes went wide at his hasty confession. "You never said…" Her smile appeared, then wavered, as an horrendous noise erupted from the adjacent bedroom.

Heavy metal music shook the very walls, and when they exited the bathroom, smoke billowed through both bedrooms. René was taking his orders very seriously.

Smoke alarms screamed, and the door to the bedroom

slammed against the wall. The cacophony was deafening.

Jack pulled Solange along the wall, hoping to encounter René and send him with her to Tournade, but he couldn't see a damned thing. Where the hell was he?

"René!" he called. "Get outside!"

No answer, or if there was he couldn't hear it. He would just have to hope that René had somehow formed his own plan of escape.

When they reached the opening to the corridor, Jack urged Solange out into the hallway and down to her knees. They scrambled to the kitchen, smoke rising above them, creating a screen.

Several men rushed past, probably headed for the bedrooms, unable to see the two of them for all the smoke.

When they got into the kitchen, Jack saw the back door standing open. Apparently the two guards stationed there were the same ones who had hurried right by him and Solange in the hallway.

Jack grabbed a meat mallet from the counter and smashed the key box. He snagged the four key rings off their hooks and shoved them into Solange's outstretched hands.

"Hurry!" he commanded, kissing her swiftly and hard and pushing her out the back door. She ran like hell.

With a brief and fervent prayer for her, he turned back to finish his mission.

He halted at the door to the room where the weapons were stored and struck the padlock with the mallet. After three blows, the aged hasp gave way.

He had just reached inside to liberate one of the automatics when an arm snaked around his neck and jerked him backward.

Jack whirled, breaking the hold, locking on the wrist of the hand that held the weapon.

They struggled for it. The gun tumbled to the floor.

"Help! Todi! Weapons room!"

The loud shout brought a clatter of footfalls on the flagstones of the smoky kitchen.

Through the noise of the scuffle, Jack tried to listen for the roar of an engine.

If he could delay them long enough, Solange would have a chance to make it.

Chapter 12

The chambering of a round alerted Jack just in time to turn, using his attacker as a shield when the second guard fired. He pushed the dead man at the shooter, plunging them both away from him.

Todi, the one who fired, fell backward, cracked his head on the sharp corner of the tiled table. Jack figured he was dead by the time he hit the floor.

The shots would bring reinforcements. Jack grabbed the Beretta out of Todi's lax fingers, checked the load and started back down the smoke-filled corridor to find René.

"Jacques!"

He turned to find Solange silhouetted in the doorway of the kitchen, car keys still in her hand.

"I heard shots! Are you hurt?"

"Get out of here!" he ordered. "Go! I'll get René."

"I'm coming with you. The garage is locked and

none of these keys fit. The only vehicle outside it is empty of petrol.''

"Stay behind me," he snapped, and headed down the corridor to the bedrooms.

The boy was on his knees near his bedroom door, coughing and trying to crawl out. Flames had engulfed the draperies and the bed. Jack stuck the pistol in the back of his belt, scooped René up and headed back out.

"Where…where is Solange? Did she get away?" René gasped. "Will she…bring the police?"

Suddenly cold metal slammed against Jack's temple. He halted, René in his arms, still gasping. Solange lay on the floor unconscious.

"*Police?* You have betrayed me!" Chari shouted, wild with fury. "Bring René in there! Into the study!"

"Are you mad? The fire!" Jack protested. "We have to get out of here now before it spreads. Take René and let me get the woman, Chari. Please!"

René was already wriggling out of his grasp. Jack released his legs so he could stand. Ignoring the threat of Chari's pistol, Jack crouched down and lifted Solange in his arms.

"To the study! All of you," Chari yelled again, prodding Jack with the gun.

When they reached it, Chari stepped around him and opened the door, the gun still positioned to blow off Jack's head.

Jack hurried through, fearing they would be trapped. The study windows were solidly barred. But not those above the ground floor in the tower, he remembered René telling him.

As soon as he could put Solange down, he would have to disarm Chari and get them the hell out of here.

"Downstairs," Chari directed. He waved the gun

dangerously as he backed to the door that led into the tower.

Jack realized the man was not in control. His eyes were wild and his hand shaking. It would be a miracle if he didn't shoot one of them accidentally.

René maneuvered his way between Jack and his father, practically breathing down Jack's collar as they descended the steps.

All the way down, Jack could hear Chari behind them, muttering and cursing to himself.

"Use your gun," René said, prodding the weapon Jack had in his belt. Take me hostage," he rasped, coughing again as he spoke. "I do not think he will—"

"Shh," Jack warned. There wasn't a damned thing he could do right now with Solange in his arms.

"Inside!" Chari demanded, pushing past them to open the door at the bottom of the stairwell.

Jack entered the laboratory. This dismal cellar was where Solange had worked, he realized, automatically scanning the lab for another exit, then remembered she had told him there wasn't one.

How he regretted he had involved her in this. A delicate little doctor with no experience in this sort of thing. What the hell had he been thinking? Now look at her. He did and noticed that her eyes were open. She was probably in shock, definitely dazed.

She raised one hand and rubbed the back of her head where Chari must have hit her with the pistol.

Jack gently set her on her feet and took her hand, squeezing it hard, then letting it go. "Be ready," he warned her in English. Chari was still aiming at them, keeping them in his peripheral vision.

There were two doors opposite the one they had entered. One was closed. At the other a very large man stood in the opening, his hands propped on either side of the door frame. Others—Jack could not see how many—were moving around inside working at something.

René was still hacking up smoke and shaking. That seemed to bring Solange back to reality. She moved closer and rested her hand on the boy's shoulder.

The fat guy had heard them enter and swerved around. "Get in here and grab a canister. We are not leaving without these containers. They are promised."

Chari issued a short bark of bitter laughter. "I'm not touching that, Belclair!"

"You know what will happen if we aren't able to deliver this!" Belclair shouted. "It is half paid for!"

Chari threw up his free hand. "Then take as many as you and the men can carry and *go!* I will meet you at the garage."

He moved closer to Belclair, the pistol still aimed in the direction of Jack, Solange and René.

"You dare give *me* orders? *You?*" Belclair spat on the floor. "You are nothing, you half-baked cinema freak! Your only value to us was in providing facilities." He snorted. "And your stupidity and greed, of course. I should kill you now, but—"

Chari raised one foot, planted it swiftly in Belclair's middle and kicked him backward through the door. His fat body crashed heavily into the others who were working inside.

Chari slammed the door shut and quickly twisted the key in the lock. "The woman was right! You are a filthy pig!" he shouted.

Jack rushed him. Chari fired. The bullet grazed Jack's shoulder. He felt the sting, instinctively halted and grabbed at the wound. By the time he recovered his balance, Chari had stepped well out of reach.

René rushed up behind Jack and slipped an arm around him as if to keep him from falling. Jack felt the boy's hand fumble at his back, felt Todi's weapon slide from inside his belt.

Could René shoot his own father? Jack devoutly hoped so, or soon they would all be trapped down here.

"Get away from him!" Chari screamed at René.

"In a moment, Father. I must check him for weapons. He might shoot you."

René moved between them, his back to Chari. He gave Jack the gun. "Do it," he whispered. "Solange is behind you. He can't hit her."

Jack needed Chari alive. They had to get the whole story about the toxin. He grabbed René and placed the barrel of Todi's nine-millimeter against the boy's head. "Put the gun down, Chari, or I will kill him."

He could barely hear his own voice for the screams, shouts and pounding from inside the locked room.

"No!" Chari's mouth trembled with the word. His panicked gaze slid to the locked door that was vibrating from blows from within.

"Father!" René cried. "Do as he says! Please, I do not want to die!"

Chari's gun wavered. He firmed his grip and stiffened his arm, bracing it with his other hand. "Let him go or I will shoot!"

"You can't do that," Jack argued. "He is your son, Chari. Your blood. Think! Who would carry on your work? He is your only hope of immortality."

"My work will stand—"

"And how will this story stand for anything if you

both die? That is what you were in this for, why you played this part, is it not? The story?''

Chari's eyes glazed a little. "It will be...told. I can—''

"How will it be told, Chari? If you shoot, so will I and you *will* die where you stand." Jack shook his head slowly. "It will end here, Chari. Only the two bad movies and a charge of treason as your epitaph. Is that what you want?''

Indecision clouded Chari's features, but he held the weapon steadfast. "They were not *bad!* No one understood them, what I was trying to say.''

"But you could do better next time. Think about it. You need that chance, Chari.''

"Father! In prison there would be time to write! To plan!'' René exclaimed. "Think of the experiences you have, the material. I will help you. Bring you supplies. Arrange everything. Together we can do it.'' He added an impressive whine. "Please do not let him kill me!''

"Get rid of that gun or I *will* shoot him, Chari,'' Jack declared in his most menacing voice.

Chari slowly lowered his arms. The gun hung useless by his side, his mind obviously elsewhere.

"Drop it on the floor, Chari. Let it go,'' Jack ordered. Smoke was drifting through the open door to the stairwell. He knew the study must be in flames by this time. Even now it might be too late to get out.

The gun thunked as it hit the floor.

Jack released René and the boy scurried forward to grab the weapon, then scrambled back beside Jack.

"What about them, sir?'' he asked, inclining his head toward the locked door. "Should we let them out?''

"We can't. We'll have to leave them. If we open it, whatever is in those canisters could spread if they were damaged. Is there another way out of here other than the study and the windows upstairs?''

René shook his head. ''Shall I tie him up?''

''No. Let's go.'' He turned toward the smoke-filled doorway, their only exit. Solange had a stack of what appeared to be lab suits in her arms. He grabbed some, threw them at René and Chari, then rushed to the sink. ''Douse these, put them over your heads, then follow me.''

Jack shrouded first Solange, then himself in the sopping fabric. ''Let's go. Solange, hang on to my belt. René, you next.''

He double-timed up the winding stairs. He had no idea where Piers and the other guards were right now. At least a couple were in that locked room with Belclair.

If the others were outside watching the chateau go up in flames, Jack doubted this escape from the tower—if indeed they were able to effect one—would matter much.

He kept his eyes shut and his hands against the walls as he climbed. When he reached the door to the study, it was closed. It was also bowed toward him and hot as hell.

He rushed on past it, vastly relieved when he reached the next door that led into one of the bedrooms. Once the four of them were inside, he slammed the door and went straight for the window and tried to open it.

Painted shut.

René grabbed a small stool and brushed Jack aside to break out the panes. He took the time to knock out the shards that might injure them climbing out.

''You go first,'' Jack ordered. ''Take your time and find good toeholds. Solange, come over here and watch how he does it. You'll go next.''

While she was approaching, René glanced past Jack at his father who was observing the boy as he readied for the perilous climb down. There was sadness in René's dark eyes, Jack noted, but also promise. The boy had meant what he had said to Chari about helping him. He knew his father was mad.

"Go ahead, son, and be careful," Jack told him. "We'll be right behind you."

He pressed Solange closer to the window so that she could see how it was done.

The descent proved easier than Jack had imagined. The old stones provided more purchase than most of the mountain faces he had climbed.

The agile René had made it without a hitch and, much to Jack's relief, so had Solange. She had kicked off her shoes and gone down the side of the tower like an expert climber. They stood on the ground and watched Chari, who had lingered longer at the window than he should have.

With less than a dozen feet left to go, he suddenly lost his hold and fell, landing squarely on both feet. One leg snapped. Chari crumpled to the grass, screaming.

"We have to get him away from the tower," Jack said. There was danger that the structure would collapse if the fire ravaged it.

The middle section of the chateau was an inferno already. Also, Piers and whoever was left of the guards could be skulking around somewhere.

With Chari screaming foul curses, the three of them lifted him and carried him to the far edge of the yard, then into the woods.

"We have to get someone out here immediately to see about containment," Jack announced. "Solange, do you still have any of those keys?"

She shook her head, raising her hands to show they were empty. Probably dropped them when Chari beaned her in the hallway. Tears were streaming from her reddened eyes. Whether from the smoke or sheer terror, Jack couldn't tell.

He brushed a hand over her face, sweeping the sooty hair away from her brow and off her cheek. "Don't cave now, sweetheart. You're doing great."

"No keys," she whispered. "What will we do, Jacques?"

"I'll have to hotwire something. René, stay here with your father until help comes," he said. He took Solange's hand and headed for the garage at a run. With Todi's pistol he fired into the wood around the padlock, then kicked out the section that held the hasp. The door swung open.

In less than four minutes he had the Land Rover, the closest vehicle to the door, up and running. "It's up to you, Solange. Get to Tournade and contact the team. Have them send backup. And cleanup," he added.

"Where will you be?" she asked as she slid behind the wheel.

"Looking for Piers. He has some of that toxin with him, and I know he hasn't left yet." He glanced around the garage. "It appears all the vehicles are still here. Looking for the keys must have delayed him, thank God.

"As determined as he was to get that stuff into Tournade, I don't think he will give up. He must have a grudge against someone in the village. Maybe the whole population, given how adamant he was about using the stuff there."

"Your shoulder's still bleeding," Solange observed. "I should see about that first."

"It's nothing and there's no time. Now get out of here!"

She obediently put the car in gear and rolled out of the garage. He watched as she took off down the driveway and disappeared around the corner of the burning mansion.

Solange, accelerator pushed to the floorboard, flew down the drive to the main road, bouncing over the ruts in the unpaved surface. She had taken the SUV and the gears were grinding. Her own car had an automatic transmission and it had been years since she had driven anything else. Using the clutch was coming back to her, however, and she relished the power in the sturdy vehicle.

She might even need the four-wheel drive before this was over. Thank goodness the Land Rover handled easily.

Once she had turned onto the highway and encountered a straight stretch of road, she glanced over her shoulder into the back seat. There were several boxes she thought might be ammunition of some kind.

She could not see what was behind the second seat in the space meant for luggage. Coming up on the twisting road that led through the low hills to the village, she had to abandon checking out the interior of the Land Rover and concentrate on her driving.

She kept glancing up at the rearview, imagining the worst, that Piers might overpower Jack and follow her. Soon a distant cloud of dust confirmed it. She knew it wouldn't be Jack on her heels. It had to be Piers on his way to Tournade.

Though the car itself was not visible, she judged it would be little more than five minutes behind her. If it was the Saab, it might very well catch up to her before she reached the village.

The wooden bridge loomed ahead, an old structure spanning the swift, narrow tributary of the Aisne River. The Rover lumbered over the bridge, and Solange cut sharply to the right, headed for the concealment of the nearby stand of trees. She pulled over a small rise and braked the car with a jarring thump. Quickly she hopped out, intending to conceal herself well away from the vehicle.

When she passed the back windows, she happened to glance inside. Dark green wooden boxes were stacked in the back. Hoping to locate a weapon of some kind to defend herself with if caught, Solange popped open the hatch and lifted the latch on one of the lids.

Weapons, for sure. Guns. Grenades. In another box there were sticks of dynamite. In another, caps and fuses. She had been riding in a car full of explosives.

There must have been plans to use more than a biological weapon to create havoc. Or perhaps this was for blowing up the chateau when they had finished the work there?

What would Jack do with these? The answer erupted out of nowhere, astounding her with its sheer insanity. But she had to do something. Jack would if he were here.

If that car behind her was the Saab, Jacques had said it was geared for great speed for their escape from the prison. She would be overtaken before getting help. But if she stayed hidden here and did nothing, it would fly right past her, reach Tournade and Piers would carry out his plan with the toxin.

If only she could destroy enough of the bridge to keep those following her from crossing to her side of it, she could at least prevent the toxin from getting to the village.

Once they had been stopped, she could hurry on to the village herself and get Jacques's team to order helicopter support from somewhere to go to the chateau and help him.

Guns were out of the question. Firearms were a total mystery to her. She knew virtually nothing about dynamite, either, or how to prepare it for use. However, she had watched enough television and movies to know that grenades were simple to operate. One pulled the pins out and the things exploded.

Timing would be critical, she guessed, but how long did it take between pulling out the pin and the actual detonation? Time enough to throw it, of course. Would enough damage occur to make the bridge impassable? It was a very old structure, hardly wide enough for two cars to pass at once, so she thought that wrecking it might be possible. However, grenades blew up, rather than down. Didn't they?

Low berms of earth rose on either side of the bridge where it connected to land. Would they protect her?

She looked down at the deadly grenades. Must she pull all of the pins or would one do the trick and detonate the rest? And where should she put them to blow up a bridge? Underneath would be best, where the supports were, of course, but there was too little time to do that.

The road wound around the low hills and she could see the car coming, now about half a mile away. Somehow she had to stop it. She dared not count on damaging the bridge enough, but perhaps she could block it.

Act! Do something or it will be too late! She ordered herself to move.

In an act of desperation, she climbed back into the SUV, spun the wheels as she backed it onto the road, then headed straight for the bridge and parked it there about a third of the way across the forty-foot span, facing the way she had come.

She leaped out, not even bothering to shut the door, and ran around and opened the hatch.

She lifted two grenades out of the box to take with her. In case this did not work, she must try to throw them at the car as it passed.

She pulled out the pin of one of those left in the box, tossed it back in and ran as fast as she could. She dived behind the berm of earth and lay flat against the ground, her hands over her ears and her face in the dirt.

Nothing happened. Seconds passed. Was the grenade a dud? Were they all?

She heard the car approaching, heard the change in the sound as it reached the bridge and left the solid surface of the road. *No! She could not let them pass!*

Solange scrambled up, a grenade in hand and dashed from behind the berm. Piers was behind the wheel of the Saab. She could see his face clearly. Another of the guards rode in the passenger seat. The Saab slowed to a crawl and was steadily pushing the SUV backward off the bridge. It was almost off. In seconds he would be able to drive around it.

She yanked the pin on the grenade she was holding and threw it at the open hatch of the SUV. Without pausing to see whether it hit its target, she leaped back behind the berm, hitting with a full length, bone-jarring thud and covered her head with her arms.

Almost simultaneously, the grenade exploded. A

larger, deafening explosion followed. Then the ground shook beneath her repeatedly.

Debris rained down, an incessant shower of it. A shard of metal impaled a clump of grass near her shoulder.

She knew she screamed, but could hear nothing now and felt absolutely numb, as if she were floating. Then she realized she was sliding. The very earth was moving under her, rocks tumbling around her. She grabbed at grass, at a nearby shrub, but it was all falling with her.

She slid free of solid ground, arms windmilling as she hit the water with a splash and sank.

A current snatched at her, towing her downstream as she fought her way to the surface. It seemed the harder she struggled, the more difficult it became to make her muscles respond. Jacques would not give up. He would never give up, she kept telling herself. And neither would she.

Wreckage swept past her. She struggled upward toward the light, sucked in a deep breath and managed to stay afloat until she broke free of the eddy. Near the steep edge of the bank, she found calmer waters and began to swim back upstream toward the bridge.

The old structure had survived, though portions of the railings on either side stuck up like broken black teeth. The Rover was nothing more than fragments, unrecognizable.

A large charred section of the other vehicle dangled, swinging precariously on one corner of the savaged rail.

She trod water and watched as it swung free and splashed down.

She had done it! It had actually worked. A bit better than she had hoped it would, she thought wryly, as she doggedly worked her way back through the water.

She began to search for a place where the bank was not too steep and overgrown with vegetation for her to climb out.

Her success was seriously marred by the fact that there was now no way for her to get to Tournade. No way to summon help for Jacques and René.

She could not let herself consider the fact that she had just killed two men. The realization of it clawed away at the edge of her mind, but she staunchly kept it at bay.

There were too many other, more critical problems left to resolve for her to dwell on any emotional trauma.

For one thing, there was the toxin Piers must have had in the car.

Chapter 13

Jack cursed the wound in his shoulder that had slowed his reaction time. He'd circled around the chateau searching for Piers until he heard René shout for him to come back.

He had seen them immediately, headed for the garage at a dead run, Piers holding one of the toxin canisters under his arm like a football.

Vincent had been running backward, firing at Jack, but his aim was bad. Jack zigzagged across the open yard, providing an erratic target.

They had outrun him and made it into the garage. Piers almost ran him over as the Saab burst from the open door and flew down the driveway.

Loss of blood had weakened Jack, caused him to fumble around like an amateur while hotwiring the one vehicle left, the vintage Mercedes Chari had used last evening. He noted the gas gauge. Half full. At least it hadn't been sitting idle for years.

But, God, was it slow! He floored the accelerator and headed after Piers.

René was waving as he passed where he had left the boy and Chari in the edge of the woods. Jack braked.

"René, go to that second tree, just there." He pointed. "Buried at the base of it or in the surrounding brush is a cell phone. If you find it, call in help." He rattled off the number for the secure line to reach the team.

He only hoped Eric had been able to place the cell phone back in the original location after the incident with Piers, or at least hadn't removed it from the bushes where Jack had tossed it.

Surely it was Eric who had taken Edouard out of the mix that day. Hopefully, he would have returned and replaced the phone, in case Jack had another chance to retrieve it.

No time to worry about that now. He had to get to Tournade. No chance of overtaking Piers while driving the antique Mercedes, but he could at least put out an all-points on the Saab once he got there.

A horrifying thought occurred. What if Piers caught up with Solange? Then he would stop. Jack was not armed but Vincent was, and Piers always carried. The keys for the Saab must have been somewhere else besides a lock box in the kitchen. That section of the mansion had been in flames. Piers and Vincent had to have escaped out the front, the only other exit not blocked.

Jack pressed the accelerator harder, though he knew the old car was giving its all already. "Damn it!" He pounded one fist on the steeling wheel. The blow seemed to trigger the fireball that billowed above the horizon in front of him.

A millisecond later he heard the blasts. More than

one. He could feel the vibration beneath the wheels of the Mercedes. "Oh, God."

Frustration eating at every nerve, Jack leaned forward, a useless attempt to hurry. He was barely doing forty miles per hour.

When the bridge came into view, his heart almost stopped. A burning skeleton of a vehicle stood on the far side of the bridge. Not the Saab, he realized. He pulled up to the edge of the bridge, climbed out and looked down the steep slope of the bank. The remains of another car poked up out of the swift shallows on the far side. He recognized the distinctive shape of the fender.

Over the sound of rushing water, he heard someone cry out.

"Solange!" he shouted as he saw her. She was struggling in the water, one arm raised, less than two hundred feet downstream. The slope of the bank on the far side was too steep for her to climb out.

He jumped.

His boots were too heavy to swim effectively. His clothing dragged him down, but there was no time to consider that. He rode the current, his weakened muscles screaming. *Hang on, hang on.* Whether he spoke to himself or to her, he didn't know.

An interminable time later he had her in his arms. She clung to him, taking them both under. He fought his way back to the surface and managed to get them close enough to the bank that he could touch bottom.

With what seemed his last ounce of strength, he lifted her up. "Grab something. Climb!" he ordered.

He stood, submerged up to his chin and watched her snake her way up the bank, prepared to catch her if she slid back down into the water. Only when he'd assured himself she was safe on level ground did he make his own attempt.

When he neared the top of the six-foot incline, her eager hands reached out to him and grasped his wrists to pull him higher. She was more hindrance than help at that point, but Jack didn't protest.

Nothing she did would ever spark an argument with him. She was alive and that was all that mattered. *All* that mattered.

He dragged himself up beside her and collapsed on the weeds and dirt, his entire body trembling with relief, pain and exertion.

"I blew up his car," Solange said in a small voice.

She was kneeling over him, those capable little hands of hers trying to roll him over, probably to check his wound.

Jack felt laughter bubble up, totally inappropriate laughter. She was a doctor. She must be horribly upset that she'd been forced to take a life. *Lives,* he thought, remembering Vincent had been with Piers. Two souls on her wonderfully naive conscience.

He couldn't seem to care about that at the moment. All he could think was that this delicate little slip of a thing had managed to stop the bad guys. He didn't know how she had done that or what she had used.

"I'm just…glad you're…alive," he gasped. "*So* incredibly glad."

Jack smiled up at her, happiness wringing every drop of exhaustion out of his body. More than anything, he wanted to make love to her, show her how proud he was of her ingenuity, her courage.

He thought briefly of the image Joe Corda had seen before all this went down, that strange premonition. *All wet and ecstatic.* That was precisely how he felt right now.

Solange was alive! She had survived.

With his good arm, he pulled her closer and kissed her soundly on the mouth. He tasted keen relief, their combined adrenaline and something else of her alone. Fear, he realized.

He pulled back and looked into her eyes. They were red-rimmed, the blue irises almost obliterated by the dilation of her pupils. "What is it, Solange? Everything's all right now. It will be fine. You're safe."

He spoke softly, gently, as he would to a frightened child, someone in shock.

She was already shaking her head, her glance darting to the river, over her shoulder to the damaged bridge. "No, Jacques. It might not be…all right." She focused on him again as she released a weary sigh and touched his face with her fingers. "Not if Piers had the toxin with him."

"Oh, God." He *had* had it. Jack had seen the canister. For a long moment they simply looked at each other. Both knew what it could mean. If the canister had broken open, if the vials had not survived, the toxin would have been released into the river. They both had been exposed.

Finally Jack spoke, his voice brusque. "Worst case, how long do you figure we have?"

Again she shook her head, an almost imperceptible shake this time. "I…I don't know. Perhaps twenty-four hours, maybe more. I attempted to destroy it in storage, but the temperature would not rise. Belclair gave me no chance to test the substance myself. I only had his notes on the findings."

She looked again toward the bridge. "Of course, the

heat of the explosion might have…or not. Perhaps it takes sustained heat to destroy it. The water might have dispersed it enough to reduce its effect on us. But it only takes a minuscule amount. I simply do not know.''

Jack reached for her, surrounding her with his arms, holding her, rocking her.

''This is so *unfair*.'' She sounded angry now.

Unfair? She still believed that any fairness existed in the world? Poor Solange. Life was chance and that was a fact. He should have expected some kind of incident, going into this mission. And he should never have allowed her to come with him. But it was too late now for self-recrimination. At least, too late to voice it. He would go to his grave with the guilt. Maybe sooner than later.

''We have had the vaccine,'' he offered hopefully.

''Yes, but that was for ricin, not this. It could prove useless.'' Tears tracked down her cheeks, melding with the water still dripping from her hair.

Jack brushed them away. ''Our luck has held so far,'' he told her. ''Look what you've done, Solange. You saved an entire village.''

Suddenly she pushed away from him and sat up straight. ''We have to let someone know right away. They will have to do something to decontaminate the water if that is possible! And René is still at the chateau. He will need help.''

''Listen,'' Jack said. He could already hear the distant whup-whup of rotor blades, though he couldn't see anything yet. ''Helicopters. René must have found the phone, or else the authorities are checking out the smoke from the fire and the explosions. In a few minutes we will have more people here than you can count.''

Even as he spoke, his words were punctuated with the whiny hee-haw of an ambulance on its way from Tournade.

She looked in the direction of the village, then back at him. "We will be quarantined. Isolated separately, I expect."

"I'm afraid so. There will be the debriefing, too. That is always done individually."

"One more kiss…for luck?" Solange suggested with a brave, teary smile.

"Many more, I promise," Jack said, sliding his hand over her wet clothes and feeling the precious, vibrant body beneath. "We will get through this, Solange."

But when his mouth met hers, desperation fueled the kiss and it was not all hers. Both of them knew it could be the last kiss they ever shared.

By the end of his second day of isolation in the secure facility just outside Paris, Jack was ready to break out and get some answers.

God only knew he had given enough of them to French intel. He had been debriefed to within an inch of his life and had nothing more to tell them. He had made his own reports for the record.

His shoulder was healing, a wound hardly worth the term. He was so full of antibiotics, his veins were probably stretched to the max. No evidence of exposure to the toxin had occurred in him so far and he knew he was almost home free in that respect.

Reaction to ricin and the like took two to three days, he knew. Respiratory distress would have been apparent by this time if he had been affected.

He had spoken briefly with Holly Amberson by telephone three times. All she had told him was that the threat was contained and they had managed to keep it out of the news to avoid public panic. She had seemed uncomfortable when he demanded to know Solange's condition and where she was being kept.

He glared at the telephone. It was a receive-only line and he could not call out. French security was determined to keep the incident under wraps at all costs. There were guards outside the locked door. No windows. No vents larger than six inches in diameter. He was effectively trapped unless he created some disturbance that would require opening the door. Even then, he was not certain they would.

The inactivity, not to mention the worry, was killing him. He lay back on the uncomfortable hospital bed and closed his eyes.

With all his might, Jack zeroed in on Eric. "Get me the hell out of here. *Now* before I kill somebody!" He even said the words out loud. Very loud.

Five seconds later the phone rang. Jack snatched it up. "You heard me, Vinland. Make it happen."

"Take it easy, Jack. Holly's on her way."

"What do you know about Solange? How is she? *Where* is she?"

"Holly will give you a full report. She's talking with the doctors right now and will be there within the hour."

Vinland's usual lighthearted tone was missing, Jack noted. He was broadcasting some bad vibes. Jack could actually feel them. Fine time for a psychic connection to kick in. It scared the hell out of him.

"Eric, be straight with me. Please. Is Solange ill? I have to know."

There were a couple of seconds silence. "Yes," he

finally admitted. "But she is alive, Jack. I can tell you that much. She's alive and she's fighting."

Fighting.

Jack couldn't speak. He replaced the receiver, set the phone on the nightstand and stared into space.

In his mind's eye, he could see her. Lying still and quiet, heavily suited nurses and doctors monitoring her every breath. Tubes, wires, machines, locked doors. And worst of all, if conscious, she would know what to expect next. She would be aware of her internal organs disintegrating and how blood would rush out everywhere.

His anguish was so profound and consuming, he was not even aware that anyone was in the room with him until he felt a hand on his shoulder and heard the voice.

"Jack? It's okay."

He could only shake his head. Nothing would ever be okay again. Not ever.

"Come on," Holly told him in her no-nonsense way. "Put some pants on and let's go see her." She unfolded a pair of jeans and a pullover shirt.

He saw that she actually meant to help him dress. "How bad?" he demanded as he snatched the clothing from her and began to put it on.

"She's holding her own right now. There's fever, but she hasn't progressed beyond regular flu symptoms."

"Bleeding?" he rasped as he shoved his feet into the loafers Holly had brought.

"None. Look, Jack, it could just be a simple case of—"

"Yeah, but we know better, don't we," he said bitterly. "I dragged her into this, knowing what could happen. Hell, I should be the one. It should have been me."

"But it's not, so give it a rest!" Holly snapped.

"Don't you think I feel responsible, too? I was the one who insisted you take her with you! And she's got to be feeling pretty stupid right about now to have black-mailed you into taking her, right? Yeah, she told me about that before she got so sick. We all feel bad about it, not just you. Get over it and give the girl some credit, will you? She felt she had to go and she went, just like you did."

"'Life's a bitch and then you die'? Is that all you've got to say?" Jack thundered.

"Sometimes, yeah, that's the way it is!" Holly exclaimed, hands on her hips and her black eyes flashing. "Now are you gonna ream me a new one all day long or you want to get out of here and go see her?"

Her expression softened. "She's been asking about you, Jack. That's why I'm here. And if you knew the threats I had to make and the strings I yanked—"

His anger deflated, melted down to something approaching grief. But it was too soon to grieve. If there was any way to save Solange, he meant to find it. He grabbed Holly's arm. "Let's go."

They didn't have far to travel. "Her room is on the floor below yours," Holly told him as they reached the elevator. "Every biomed expert in the country and a few choice imports have been working around the clock on all of you."

"All?" Jack asked as he punched the down button repeatedly. "Who else besides Solange and me?"

"Belclair survived the fire. The tower was mostly stone and never ignited. The two guys locked in with him suffered smoke inhalation, but the separate ventilation system in the tower saved them."

"René?" Jack asked. Solange, especially, would want to know he was all right.

"Checked out okay. He's staying at his digs over on the Left Bank and he's been driving us nuts! You gave him our secure number and he's used the hell out of it. Calls constantly wanting to know how you and the doctor are doing. You need to have a word with that kid when you get time."

She led the way out as the elevator stopped. Jack would have pushed right past her, but she stopped him with a hand on his arm.

"Jack, I'm sorry if it looks like we've been stone-walling you. We were advised to wait until we knew whether you'd succumb to this, too, before we told you anything."

He ignored the apology. "Which room is she in?"

Holly pointed to the closed door on her right. "This is the observation room. First, I think you should—"

"Hell with that."

Solange wasn't contagious. She'd been poisoned. And he didn't have any bug that would make her worse or his doctors would have discovered it.

He shoved Holly aside and entered the door next to the one she had indicated.

The sight that greeted him stopped him cold when he stepped inside. Solange lay motionless as a marble statue, an oxygen mask over her face and IVs in both arms.

She looked so small, so defenseless. So pale. An attendant, eyes wide over her close-fitting mask raised a gloved hand to wave him back, but Jack ignored her.

He approached the bed, took Solange's nearest hand in both of his and stood there, helpless to do anything.

Dimly he was aware of the nurse dragging a chair

closer to the bedside and urging him to sit down. He did, his eyes never leaving Solange. This was his watch to keep.

"Any further development?" Will asked as he entered the observation room. His dark gaze flew to the one-way window where Holly sat watching Jack and the patient.

"No bleeding. That's something. Blood pressure's low and her fever's still way too high, but she's holding her own." She sighed. "Look at him, Will. If she dies, he's not gonna get over it."

"He got over Maribeth," Will argued. "Jack's tough."

"No, he didn't get over it, you goof. He still blames himself for that and he wasn't even involved in the mission that killed her. But I can't argue logically that he's not partly responsible for this, and we both know it. Besides, I think he really loves this one."

"C'mon, he loved his wife," Will argued, leaning against the edge of the window.

"Yeah, well, in a way I guess he did. But they were more buddies, I think. Or partners."

"Like us," Will said, nodding.

Holly looked up at him but didn't answer. It hadn't been a question. She wished it were. "This is different with him, though, I can tell. The little doc really got to him in a big way. They were lovers. That's pretty clear."

"I don't know how you can possibly tell that. Anyway, it's none of your business, Holly," Will warned. "Stay out of it. Why did you let him go in against doctor's orders?"

"She needs him there. Nobody wants to die alone."

Will turned and pierced her with a look. "This is not like you, Holly."

She shook her head. "The whole mission has creeped me out from the get-go. Give me a hail of bullets anyday. What's the latest on Chari?"

"Singing like a canary on speed. We can't shut him up. Eric and Joe are scrambling to keep up with the transcripts of his confession. And—get this—the fool wants copies."

"Yeah, he would. What's the word on Belclair?"

"His respiratory problems are much worse. Nothing's showing up in his blood, but they're doing further tests. He's asthmatic, so they aren't sure whether it's that, exacerbated by smoke and stress, or if it's the toxin."

"I *hope* it's the toxin," Holly declared fervently. "I hope the son of a bitch dies *today!* He deserves it."

She released a worried sigh as she looked through the window. "If Belclair lives, I'm afraid of what Jack might do next."

Will paused on his way to the door and gave her shoulders a fond squeeze. Holly closed her eyes and relished the touch. Given this past week and a half, she badly needed a bear hug, but she could hardly ask him for that.

When she looked up at him, he gave her a bracing smile. "Keep a close eye on him, Holly. Jack's not himself right now. And don't you worry, we'll take care of everything else that's going on."

"Thanks…partner," she said, but the door was already closing behind him. The man wasted no time where some things were concerned.

Holly turned back to the window. "Girl, I sure hope your luck holds out," she whispered to Solange. "You might have used it all up finding some guy to love you that much."

Chapter 14

Solange felt the tremors in her body increase. She figured she was probably dying. Her eyes would not open. No energy left.

''No!'' someone exclaimed. She wanted to argue, but perhaps she was wrong. She couldn't seem to care.

Who would miss her? Father? She smiled at that. Yes, he would wonder who would take his suits for dry cleaning and bring them home again. Who would pay Marie for cleaning their house, cooking their meals? Who would wake him in time to go to bed at a decent hour when he fell asleep in his chair?

Someone else should have been doing that for years, she thought dreamily. Marie herself would do it for nothing extra. A ring, perhaps.

Solange longed to fly free, see what came next. Her head ached, pulsed so fiercely she could hardly hold a thought. Poison had invaded her system and it was shutting down, failing her. She wished she were stronger, but all her fight was gone.

She kept waiting for the rush, the expulsion of her life force. Would she wing up to the ceiling as one patient said he had done briefly before coming back? Would she see the ones who tended her hovering over her lifeless body?

Someone squeezed her hand. It seemed she could feel the very whorls on the pads of his fingers as they pressed against her palm. Painful, but sweet. Jacques? Would he be here or had he gone already? She forced out a whisper. "Jacques?"

"Here, Solange. I'm here."

His breath touched her cheek. A good warmth.

"Solange, the fever is less. Two whole degrees in the past hour."

But it was not the fever that killed. The heart was the thing. Solange concentrated, trying to feel the beat within her chest. Too weak, she supposed, feeling nothing.

"Don't give up," his voice pleaded. Not like Jacques. He did not plead. Not that man. He demanded. "Don't you give up, Solange!" Ah, yes, there it was, the order. Firm. Comforting. Something predictable in all this. He would never change.

Shivers shook her violently. "Cold," she cried, hoping for more cover, something…

"Sweat. It's breaking," someone said. She tried to nod.

"Pressure's dropping." She knew that. All her senses turned inward now, she coasted on her knowledge, tried to focus. But reason slipped away, just out of reach.

"Code…!" someone cried, a harsh sound, one she

recalled too well. Jacques's hand tore away from hers, leaving her fingers, her hand, bereft.

There was a scurry of activity. She could hear the clink of metal, a commotion, but it faded into nothing.

A jolt shook her hard as if she'd been yanked through a force field. A thousand pricks of energy shot through her, touching every cell. She heard a rapid, then steady, blip that was so familiar.

"She's back." Someone sounded relieved. Solange only felt disgruntled and uncomfortable, her body still tingling with the shock.

The hand was holding hers again. Jacques's hand. She clung.

When she woke again, Solange managed to open her eyes enough to see through a tangle of lashes. She felt fairly lucid, remembered where she had been brought by the helicopter and why. She noted the location had not changed. She also noticed she had company.

The large, tanned hands she loved still encompassed one of hers. Near their joined hands, Jacques rested his head against the shiny metal railing of the bed. She wanted to touch his hair, to feel her fingers slide through it as she had when they made love.

She wanted to make love again, she realized, and would have laughed at herself if she could have summoned the strength. All she could manage was a soft sound, something between a cough and a groan.

His head came up immediately and his eyes met hers. "You're awake. Thank God." Despite the fatigued look on his face, his smile looked euphoric.

She tried to smile back.

"You're going to make it, Solange. Temp's down, pressure's up, heart's steady. I knew you wouldn't give up. I told them how strong you really are."

She watched, fascinated, as a tear slowly tracked down and got caught in the stubble on his cheek.

"How…long?" Her voice sounded hollow, far away when she spoke.

"Sixty-eight hours since the onset," he told her. "They say seventy-two's the magic number, I know, but you're already home free. Everything looks great. *You* look great." He glanced at the door. "Your father's here. He'll need to see you awake."

Instead of leaving as she expected he would, Jacques raised a cord and pushed the buzzer. "Send in Dr. Micheaux's father, please."

Not a request, but another command. Solange's shaky smile widened. Father wouldn't like that summons. *He* was Dr. Micheaux, not Dr. Micheaux's *father*.

Jacques was probably running the hospital by now. How she would miss him when he left to go home to America. That would be soon, she supposed. The mission must be completely over by now, everything settled, all danger abolished.

She wanted to ask, but that would wait. Her father had come in to stand just behind Jacques. He looked rather shell shocked. Then she remembered his accident. His thick silver hair had lost its gleam and for once in his life, appeared unkempt. How much smaller he seemed to her than when she had last seen him. She tried to smile.

"Papa," she managed. "How is your head?"

He was still a handsome man, just shy of sixty, his regular features hardly lined by the years. However, the carefully composed expression he usually wore, the one that concealed all emotion, vanished. His face seemed to age and crumple as she watched. Tears streaked down his face. "My sweet angel," he rasped.

Solange cut her gaze to Jacques to see his reaction. He had moved to one side to allow her father to come closer, but he still held her hand. He seemed to notice that, too, and gently put it, palm down on the bed.

"I suppose I should go," he said with a halfhearted shrug.

"Goodbye, Jacques," she said. Though her lips moved, she heard no sound emerge. As farewells went, she would have wished for a little more. At least a kiss. He once said that he loved her.

Her father took Jacques's place at her side, but Solange had lost the heart for attempting conversation. She had lost her heart altogether. It was walking out the door with Jacques Mercier and going with him wherever he went. And he didn't even know.

Holly joined him as he came out into the corridor. "You look like hell."

He grinned at her. "Yeah, but I feel great. Did you see? She was smiling. Her eyes were open and she was smiling."

"Yeah, you can relax now. She's out of the woods. Why don't you grab a shower and a quick nap?"

Jack immediately sensed something was wrong. "Spill it, Holly. What's up?"

She rolled her eyes and expelled a sharp sigh. "How do you *do* that? A body would think you're psychic or something."

"Yeah, but we know better, don't we? Tell me what's wrong." He walked with her to the deserted sitting area adjacent to the nurses' station. She plunked down wearily and patted the chair beside her. Jack took it, waiting expectantly.

"Belclair's gone."

"Gone?" Jack repeated in disbelief. His mind couldn't seem to grasp that they had lost something akin to the size of a small rogue elephant.

She nodded. "We had to turn him over to the French. Don't ask me why they risked moving him, but they were transferring him to another facility. The guards who were transporting him are missing. The ambulance attendant is dead. Shot twice at close range."

"Damn." Jack rubbed the back of his neck where the muscles were beginning to scream. "Assemble the team. We need a game plan. Meantime, where can I go to get my head on straight?"

"Got a room for you just down the hall. I think it has everything you'll need."

Not everything, Jack thought. More than anything, he needed to stay close to Solange, but that was going to be impossible until Belclair was apprehended.

His whole concept of the enemy had changed since beginning this mission. They were no longer a faceless entity. They had become people with different agendas and personalities. Some were shallow like Chari, some dedicated, some inherently evil and others, the hired guards, simply sucked into the venture by chance.

He seemed to be relating to everyone differently than before. No more herding people into categories. Friends or enemies, that simply was not working anymore.

Jack's team remained a cohesive unit where the job was concerned, but he had to admit that each had established a bond with him that had nothing to do with the work. If anything happened to any one of them, he would have lost someone unique. His wall of objectivity had serious breaches.

As director of Sextant, Jack had to assume control of the mission again and focus his full attention and energy on that. Technically the team had done the job they'd been brought here to do, but Belclair had escaped the French. While that was not the fault of Sextant, they could hardly leave that string dangling. It was more like a fuse that could lead to explosions just as deadly as those originally planned.

An hour later Jack, Holly, Eric, Joe and Will were gathered in one of the hospital conference rooms. He was standing at the head of the table, slightly embarrassed about how out-of-touch-he had been for the past three days. However, he knew if he had it to do over, he wouldn't change a thing. Solange had needed him. She had almost paid the ultimate price for this mission. He only wished he could have done more for her.

He would dedicate this effort to her. Get the job done. Make the world a little safer for Solange. "Okay, what have we got so far?"

"Belclair was the catalyst," Holly offered. She looked to Eric for his report.

"The three—Belclair, Piers Malfleur and Chari—were all natives of Tournade. While growing up, they were apparently treated as outcasts by the locals," Eric stated, looking at his notes. "Belclair, because he was so ungainly, a real egghead and all-round geek. By the way, that description is compliments of their esteemed peer, Tournade's current mayor."

"How did we miss finding this connection before?" Jack asked, careful to include himself in what amounted to an accusation.

"Malfleur changed his name when he left for Paris. His father was a convicted murderer, his mother a barmaid with plenty of extracurricular activities. Piers took a lot of flak about that when he was a kid. Made him an outcast. Belclair we didn't know about until Solange gave us his name. We had identified Piers when he was seen in the village, but thought he was just someone Chari had hired from local talent.''

"And Chari? Racial conflict?"

Eric cocked one eyebrow and looked over his glasses at them. "He was the outlander, the only kid in town of Middle-Eastern descent. Nobody but the girl he eventually married accepted him, and her family was not keen on the match."

"So the three banded together," Jack said. "So much for motive."

Holly held up a finger.

"Something to add regarding that?" Jack asked.

"Their motives diverged," Holly said. "Chari was in it for the money. Piers wanted Tournade wiped out, right down to the last person. Considering all that stuff Solange found in the SUV, he was planning to poison as many as possible at the festival, then wreak some serious havoc afterward. But our little doc took his vehicle and then put a period to his existence." She smiled. "Is she cool or what?"

Jack nodded, shoving the swell of remembered terror aside to deal with later. "What about Belclair? He's the one we need a fix on right now."

Eric turned to Corda. "Joe and Martine did the background on him."

Joe had the floor. "Belclair has a greedy streak, too, but he has an ax to grind with humanity. Nobody *anywhere* ever liked him. We couldn't find a soul in any of his schools, among any of the people who had ever known him who would have spit on him if he was on fire."

"Well, somebody did, and we had better find him

pretty damn quick. He's the one with the power to re-construct this nightmare,'' Jack said. ''Any leads at all?''

Will spoke up. ''Solange is our best bet, Jack. She worked with him in the lab.''

Jack was already shaking his head. ''She's not up to it yet.''

''Don't deny her this, Jack,'' Holly said, employing that motherly tone of hers. ''Solange has been as ded-icated to this as any one of us. If you leave her out of it now, she's gonna be so pissed.''

Jack shot her a warning look and she held her hands, palms up, as if backing off. As if she would.

''All I'm saying is let's give the girl a chance to offer her input.'' Her eyes narrowed. ''And allow one of *us* do it, okay?''

Jack considered what she said. His protective in-stincts toward Solange warred with what he knew must be done. ''I'll talk to her.''

Holly scoffed. ''Yeah, I can hear that now. 'Sweetie pie, you know anything? Didn't think so, okay, rest now.'''

''Not funny,'' Jack grumbled, but he felt a laugh threaten. Holly knew him too well. ''Okay, I'll let Eric interview her. He might pick up what's running through her head that she's too exhausted to say.'' He looked at each of them. ''Anything else? No? Okay, let's roll.''

They marched in force back to the wing where So-lange lay recovering from her trauma. Jack hated to dis-turb her, but he knew Holly was right. When they reached the corridor outside her room, he almost had to restrain himself from rushing inside. Instead he watched Eric do so.

"You coming in to watch?" Holly asked as she and the rest filed into the observation room.

He shook his head. "No, it's better if I don't. Maybe I shouldn't see her again until this is taken care of." He smiled, knowing he must look a little sheepish. "She sort of screws up my focus."

Holly feigned surprise. "Really? Now I never would have noticed that if you hadn't told me, boss."

Eric exited the room almost immediately. "Her old man ran me out. He's scary as hell for a little guy. She's sedated, anyway. Sound asleep. We'll have to wait until morning."

"That's all right. It would take some time for Belclair to assemble a lab and recreate any of the toxin, and all that he made before has been accounted for, right?"

"Roger that," Eric said with a succinct nod. "And the waters have tested okay downstream from the bridge, too. They think that it dispersed enough that it's no longer a danger."

Only it hadn't dispersed quite quickly enough, Jack thought, grinding his teeth. Solange had either gotten it there or Belclair had infected her on purpose back at the lab. They might never know for sure. The important thing was that she was recovering. His relief was almost debilitating.

Jack left the others and retired to the room down the hall that Holly had arranged for him, stretched out on the bed and covered his eyes with his arm to block out the light from the window.

Damn, but he was too tired to think straight. The fate of thousands might rest on their apprehension of Belclair, and he was just too exhausted to perform.

How had this happened? How had he let himself get

so wrapped around the axle about Solange that he had
to let someone else take the lead in the investigation?

He was too involved and he knew it. She was the
most serious breach in what he had termed his wall of
objectivity. He could not for the life of him imagine a
category in his life where Solange Micheaux would
comfortably fit. One of his lovers? She was that, but
she was also much, much more.

He worried that he had bottled up his deep feelings
for people for so long that now they had all broken free
and converged on this one woman. But why now? Why,
on this intensely critical mission, had Solange's well-
being zoomed to first on his list of priorities?

He needed to get a grip on reality here, repeat his
first rule: expect collateral damage and get over it.

That just seemed like heartless justification for failure
now.

Never once had he put one person above the job. Not
even Maribeth. Of course, she had always shared his
views about that. He wished he could apologize to her,
tell her how much he regretted that he had not put her
first when he should have. But she wouldn't understand,
even if he could say that to her. She had never thought
of him first, either. It probably had never occurred to
her, just as it hadn't to him. Until now.

Would Solange think that way? She was a doctor,
sworn to save lives, dedicated to humanity. Small doubt
that her job would be of primary importance to her. And
it should be. How could he expect anything else?

His thoughts raveled at the edges and finally disin-
tegrated altogether as a dreamless sleep overtook him.

It was a new day, a new chance at life. Solange
couldn't help but be happy about that. However, the

situation with regard to Jacques's mission was dire. Belclair was missing.

"A field," she told Eric after he had explained about Belclair's escape. "He mentioned that the type of flower he was using for the extract grows near Tournade. Cultivated, I would think." She watched him make a note.

She really felt so much better this morning it was amazing. Already she was sitting up halfway, propped against pillows. One of the sisters had combed her hair and given her chipped ice to crunch. The doctor had promised she could try to walk a bit later in the day. And tomorrow she would have food.

The greatest evidence that she was improving rapidly was this visitor. Eric Vinland, the one to whom she had passed the handkerchief with the information. Her contact. Now consulting with her about Belclair.

She was still involved with Jacques's mission. It bothered her a little that he was not the one asking her these questions, but at least he would know she was helping.

"It will be a local crop of genquist," she went on to explain. "You must find and watch the field. If Belclair plans to make more of the toxin, he will have to have that. I do not believe he has any other source."

"Brilliant. Absolutely brilliant," Eric said. "Now then, what do the plants look like?"

She watched him prepare to write down her description, his pen poised over the small writing pad. "I have no idea. Find a botanist."

He laughed and clicked the pen, tucking it away in his pocket. "I'll bring you a sprig when we find it."

"No, thank you, I believe I have had enough."

He winked and shook his finger at her. "Sense of

humor. I like that. Okay, I'm out of here now. You get well, Doc.''

"Eric?" she said as he reached the doorway.

He turned, eyebrows raised in question.

"Good luck."

His smile was wicked. "Uh-uh, that's not what you were thinking."

"Not exactly," she admitted. "What are you? A mind reader?"

"Me? If I were, I would know that you wanted to make pork chops out of Chari at the party that night, right?"

Her mouth dropped open.

He went on. "And I would know that right now you'd trade your retirement fund for an hour with Jack before he leaves. Oh, and he wouldn't care about that ugly hospital gown. He wouldn't mind a bit."

She snapped her mouth shut, narrowed her eyes and glared at him. What could she say? Nothing half as scathing as what she was thinking at the moment.

He shrugged. "Hey, chill, Doc. It's part of my charm. As ol' Popeye used to say, 'I yam what I yam.'"

"You are nothing but...an adolescent *eavesdropper!*"

"Don't forget *voyeur*. I see things, too."

"Do not *dare* to tell him my thoughts!" she warned.

"Popeye? I never talk to sailors."

Before she could think of a retort, he was gone. How could she ever have thought he was charming? How could he have known? Was it possible he really had been able to—

No, of course not, but if he could—and he had known about the pork chop thing and her worry about the gown just now—how horribly embarrassing was that? And perhaps convenient? Yes, it could be.

She was still delirious, that was it. Or it was her meds. What the devil had they given her?

Hopefully Eric would ignore her silly protest and tell Jacques how much she longed to see him. It did not take a psychic to guess that much was true. It was probably written all over her face.

They were going after Belclair. Despite the man's unwieldy size and sedentary habits, Solange feared he could be dangerous in more ways than the one they knew about. Then there were those people who must have helped him to escape. They were sure to be heavily armed.

What if she never had the chance to see Jacques again?

She grabbed the buzzer and pushed it with her thumb until one of the sisters came rushing in.

"The man who was just in here. Could you please call him back," she ordered.

"I am sorry, Dr. Micheaux. He and his friends have already left. They were waiting for him beside the elevator."

She started out, then stopped and turned around. "Perhaps I could telephone downstairs and have someone stop them. It might not be too late."

"No," Solange told her. "That will not be necessary. What they have to do is very important. It would be wrong of me to delay them."

Now she did not feel well. Not well at all.

Chapter 15

"Intel's heard that there's another lab." Holly tossed the report from French intelligence across the table to Jack. "Bérard says they'll handle this one, but he's going to wait until dark to raid it. Told me we should back off now and go home."

"That's gratitude for you," Jack said, thumbing through the three-page document.

"He wants the glory. The lab's right here in Paris, smaller than the one at Chari's place, according to the source. They've had a fermentor, water tank, holding tank, two sets of gas cylinders and various other weird stuff delivered there in the past two days. The genquist's probably there, too, by now. I'd say they're almost set to go into production."

"So that's why most of the genquist was gone before we found it."

For three long days and nights after locating the genquist, the team had staked out the small plot of land near the chateau where the stuff had been growing. No one had shown up, probably because there was very little left to harvest. Finally, in frustration, they had destroyed what was left of the plants and come to Paris to compare notes with their French counterparts.

Jack planned to go out to the hospital to see Solange as soon as everyone reported in. Though he had not talked with her personally, he had touched base with her doctors several times a day since he had been gone. Now that she was almost well and they had both had the time and distance to think about things, they needed to talk. However, given what Holly had brought in just now, the visit might have to wait a few more hours.

Holly dragged out one of the chairs and collapsed in it, leaning back and rubbing her forehead as if it ached. "Belclair's the only one we know about who's working with the stuff. Best guess is that someone was harvesting the plant even before he escaped, probably on his orders. Unfortunately, the locals didn't monitor conversations with his visitors or the phone calls he supposedly made to set up legal counsel. He definitely had help with that and also with the escape. Three guesses who that would be."

"The client's involved," Jack declared. "According to Chari, the EIJ has a sizable investment to protect." He tapped his pen on the folder. "Egyptian Jihad, Al-Qaeda's little brother," Jack said. "We have all we need. Time to kick ass and take names. Where's the lab located, exactly?"

"Truck driver's home, out in one of the suburbs," Holly told him. "The lab's in a trailer, a mobile unit like the ones found in Iraq. The set-up inside these is usually primitive at best, but easily relocated and difficult to trace. We simply lucked out. A neighbor got suspicious and kept up surveillance until he was sure what it was. He's retired army, a career guy.''

"We'll move as soon as everyone gets here. So the locals aren't moving on this until tonight?"

Holly shook her head. "Intel's still *coordinating*," she said with a smirk. "The stuff will be packaged and shipped to its destination before they get their act together.''

Jack and Holly were meeting in one of the larger rooms at a three-star hotel off Rue Jardin. It was a comfortable, out-of-the-way family-run establishment and totally secure. Will had seen to that. He and Eric were now at the embassy, coordinating with their contact there. Joe and Martine were closing out business in Tournade and bringing the equipment to Paris.

Jack answered the knock on the door, knowing who it was before he opened it. Eric pushed past him into the room, obviously upset. Will followed, more calmly, but his expression was no less grim. "What now?" Jack asked.

"Belclair's dead. His body was discovered dumped in an alley over on the Left Bank. They found him early this morning," Will said.

Jack had his phone out and was already punching the number of the hospital. He would need to station extra guards on Solange. She had worked with the chemist. If the EIJ knew she had been assisting Belclair, they would—

"Too late, Jack," Will told him. "They've already got her."

Damn! Jack clenched his eyes shut and warned himself not to panic. She would be okay. Solange was their ticket to recreating the toxin, or so they would be thinking.

"Let me guess," he said. "Belclair's death was not due to natural causes."

"It was the toxin," Eric confirmed. "Maybe one of the containers was damaged and he came in contact with it when he was locked in that storage room in the tower. They estimate he's been dead for two days."

And now the terrorists, probably the real hardcore fanatics, had kidnapped Solange.

An unexpected calm settled over Jack. He had felt it before. His brain sometimes shifted gears of its own accord when worse came to worst and he found himself against a wall. Instead of panic, there rose a deadly reserve of energy, coiled and ready to strike with full force. He turned to each of his team present. "Check your weapons."

He could feel their readiness, tune in on their every move and see it before they made it. When they reached the site, that empathy would extend to the enemy, he knew. This was his gift, as elusive and unpredictable as Eric's telepathy and Joe's precognition. It had evaded him at Chari's during that confrontation. Perhaps he had not needed it then as much as he did now.

The ride through the streets of Paris was silent and swift. Will drove with his usual flair, matching the speed of the local drivers without employing suicidal tactics, and neatly avoiding theirs.

When they reached the area, he ordered Will to park two blocks away. "Want me to call for backup?" Will asked.

"No."

They approached the house from the rear. Jack could

see the top of the trailer. "Get a fix on Solange if you can, Eric."

"Inside the van or truck or whatever it is. The girl must believe in me! She's broadcasting like Radio Free Europe. But she's not alone. One guy inside."

"Thanks. Holly, you and Will take the front of the house. Eric, cover the back. Don't approach. Find cover and stay well away. They'll have automatics and maybe worse." Jack shucked off his suit coat and removed his tie. "If anyone shows after I make my move, take them down any way you can. No rules."

He watched until they were in place. Then he walked up to the back of the trailer and knocked. "Another delivery. Open up," he called in colloquial Arabic. He wasn't fluent, but he had the basics down pat with a good accent.

No one answered. He repeated the words, injecting weary impatience and adding a curse.

He heard the creak of a latch and the double doors began to open. The crack opened about a foot. Jack stood where only his arm could be seen from inside and held up a small box he had picked out of a trash bin on their way down the alley. A dark brown hand reached out to take it. Jack grabbed the wrist and yanked for all he was worth.

The man's head cracked against the edge of the metal door as he fell. The Uzi he held in his free hand spat a few wild rounds before he hit the dirt. Jack pressed him to the ground, a knee in the back as he disarmed him. A blow to the head with a closed fist took care of any resistance.

"Solange?" he called. "You alone in there now?"

"Jacques!" She flung the door wide and fell into his arms.

"Thank God you're all right. You *are* all right?" He slid his hand through her hair and cupped her head, holding it against his chest. "They didn't hurt you, did they?"

"No, I'm fine. I knew you would come for me." She sounded breathless, excited.

Gunfire erupted from inside the house. "Get back in the trailer," he ordered, "behind some barrier if there is one." Jack lifted her quickly and pushed her back in. Then he scooped up the Uzi and sprayed the back door of the house.

Eric put a few rounds through the only window facing the backyard.

When Jack reached the back door, he kicked it open, wheeling to one side as it slammed inward. It was a small dwelling. He heard the scuffle of feet and loud shouts in Arabic.

Eric joined him and they went in. The nest had emptied. Whoever had been in the house, several by the sound of it, had just escaped out the front door. They heard shots.

He and Eric backed out, not wanting to risk getting hit by friendly fire.

"I'll work around to the front," Eric shouted. "Go ahead and see about Solange and the lab."

Jack was already on his way back to the trailer. The man he had pulled out of it was still on the ground, unconscious. He stepped over him and climbed in. Solange had wedged herself in between two heavy metal tanks. "Smart girl," he said. "You still okay?"

She smiled up at him and held out a hand for him to help her to her feet. "Better than okay now that you are here."

"Anything in here need immediate destruction?" he asked.

"No. They had no idea what to do with all of this. I have been delaying them by requesting unnecessary ingredients."

"You're a genius." He laughed and pulled her up and into his arms. His hands were too full, the Uzi in one, his pistol in the other. She didn't seem to mind. "You'd better wait in here a little longer while I see about…things outside."

"You'd better go. But have a care!" She gave him a little shove of encouragement and then resumed her position between the tanks.

Jack hurried back out for the cleanup. Holly had two at gunpoint, marching them back to where Jack stood waiting. Will and Eric were dragging another from the side of the house. "He aimed at Holly," Will explained. "I had to shoot him, but he'll live to talk."

"I said no rules."

"We missed one," Holly told Jack. "He leaped over the fence while I was busy with this guy. He's long gone by now."

"I think not," Will said with a short laugh. "Would you look at that."

They all turned in unison to see a white-haired fellow, stooped with age, cradling an M-16 rifle. It was pointed at a much younger man who staggered in front of him, hands clasped on top of his dark, close-cropped head. His mouth was bleeding.

"What do you make of the old guy? The neighbor who did the reporting?" Eric asked.

"Undoubtedly." Jack went forward to meet him while Eric took over guarding the prisoner he had brought them. "Good day, sir. We came to give you a hand."

"It took you long enough," the old man grumbled. "We will need this." He pulled a large roll of duct tape from his jacket pocket.

He did not identify himself. Nor did he ask who they were. He simply laid down the rifle very carefully and began to bind the prisoner he had furnished. Jack and the others followed suit.

Solange peeked out the back of the truck. Jack motioned her to join them.

When all the terrorists were securely bound hand and foot, Jack spoke to the neighbor. "The police should be here shortly. When they come…"

"I know. You were never here," the old guy said, shaking his head. "Cloak-and-dagger, just like in my war." He shooed them with a flap of one gnarled hand. "You can leave now."

"You don't understand. It's all right if—"

Again he motioned them away. "I said I will manage. Go on with you. Disappear."

Jack glanced at the others who were barely restraining their laughter. "Should we?"

"The perps will squeal," Holly said.

The old man's wrinkles folded up to form a wily grin. "No one will believe them over a decorated veteran." He pulled back his vest to reveal an impressive row of medals.

Will clicked on the safety and handed over his Beretta. "You might need this to match the bullet in that guy if anyone questions who shot him."

The fellow nodded, reverently palming the sleek 9mm.

Jack lifted Solange in his arms, and they all walked

the two blocks to where they had left the sedan parked. As soon as they were inside, Eric whooped and that set them all off. Even Solange laughed.

Jack kissed her, still too overcome with relief to discuss her abduction in detail. She clasped his arm, but seemed more glad to see him than upset by her ordeal. At the moment she looked pink-cheeked and happy. Healthy. Alive. He laughed again.

Will gunned the motor and expertly shot them through the maze of Paris streets, deftly dodging the other speed demons.

Finally the others quieted enough for Jack to make a phone call. He dialed the number for the agent Holly had spoken with earlier and who had furnished the report about the trailer lab.

"M'sieu Bérard? Are you planning to do anything about that laboratory today?" Jack asked conversationally. "If so, we are ready to assist."

"That will not be necessary." The voice was haughty as hell. "You and your people have done all that is required. We will take care of this ourselves. I am notifying your director that your mission is complete."

"Fine. So it is. Well, good luck," Jack said and rang off. He smiled at the others. "The newspapers, then the police, or vice versa?"

"Call CNN," Will said with a grin. "They'll beat everybody there."

Eric rubbed his palms together. "Old dude's gonna be famous. I can't wait for the evening news."

Jack handed him the phone. "Be my guest. Tell the world."

Solange emerged from her bath and toweled off. Refreshed, feeling like a brand-new person, she looked around the room where she had slept away a good portion of her life, the refuge she had returned to after her internship. The ice-blue and ecru, tastefully incorporated by a decorator, now looked incredibly bland and uninteresting. A cocoon from which she had emerged.

In the past two weeks the nightmare had become her reality. This safe place she had known all her life seemed more like the dream.

How strange it felt to be home again among her own things. How disappointing, knowing Jacques was no longer under the same roof with her. Of course, she understood that he had reports to make, that he had business to finish. Though he had promised to come later for the celebration her father insisted upon, Solange expected that he intended tonight to be their farewell.

She walked naked to the dressing room and thumbed through the hangers that held her wardrobe. It wasn't extensive, by any means, but for one who had existed with one ensemble and a few borrowed items for so long, it seemed excessive. Yet nothing in here appealed. Her looks had always proved a disadvantage to her in her chosen profession, so she had made it a point to dress ultraconservatively. Now her carefully selected clothes did not seem to suit her any longer.

Perhaps she was bolder than she had been. Certainly she had changed. Tonight called for something daring. With a sigh, she pulled out the most provocative thing she owned. No. Jacques should not remember her always in this basic black cocktail dress with its sensible matching pumps. Basic would not do. Perhaps Givenchy would deliver.

If there was one thing Jacques Mercier had taught her since forcing his way into her life, it was to use every ounce of her potential. She smiled to herself. He had given her a broader vision of the world, pulled the butterfly free, kicking and screaming, and there was no way she could fold up those wings.

The party commenced at six o'clock that evening. Jack noted that the elder Dr. Micheaux and his housekeeper, the lovely Marie, had pulled out all the stops.

Jack had spent the last few hours arranging for shipping home the equipment the team had brought with them and making his report for the director. Now he had arrived just in time to catch the tail end of the television newscast everyone was watching in the salon.

Everyone but Solange. She was nowhere in sight.

Holly, Will and Eric were already here. Joe and Martine had declined. They were flying to Italy tonight for their belated honeymoon, postponed because of the urgency of the mission. René Chari, wearing a rumpled tuxedo, sat cross-legged on the floor nearest the television.

Onscreen Jack recognized the gentleman introduced by the newscaster as Sergent-Chef Eugene Cholet. The old fellow, decked out in a uniform two sizes too large for him and drooping with medals, was being lauded for alerting the authorities to a "possible terrorist cell." When the anchor praised him for capturing five armed individuals before the police arrived, he merely shrugged and growled that anyone might have done it. That the lab meant to produce bioweapons was not mentioned.

Champagne flowed freely, and the music was a generational mix that added even more sparkle to the gathering. Jack was impressed with the surroundings.

Solange had grown up wealthy, he noted. And probably coddled. The creature comforts, he could provide for her, but his job would require that he be away from home much of the time. What kind of offer would that be?

Of course, he had no business offering her anything. She had a well-established career, a father who doted on her and most likely tons of friends who would miss her if she left.

It was the first time Jack had consciously considered asking her to come with him when he went back to the States, but he knew now that it had been at the back of his mind since the night they made love.

René Chari approached, switching a full glass for Jack's empty one. "You think you will be leaving soon?" he asked.

"Very soon," Jack affirmed, taking a sip of the fresh bubbly. He wished it were Scotch.

"Not for a few weeks, surely," René said with a sly grin. "You would not wish to miss the big wedding."

Jack raised an eyebrow. "Oh? Who's getting married?"

"You, if you have any sense."

The fresh remark should have made him angry, but Jack accepted it with a nod. He understood how René felt about Solange. She had been his protector at first, and since his recovery he had come to see her as a mother figure, a damsel in distress and—given that he was seventeen and all hormones—probably entertained more than a little lust for her.

Jack could hardly blame him for that. Except for the protective-mother image, he felt pretty much the same way about her himself.

They both loved her. René's feelings must be nearly

as strong as his own, since the boy was willing to relinquish her to Jack in hopes of her finding happiness.

He smiled at René. "I am humbled that you think she would have me. But she'd be a fool to give up all of this, don't you think?"

The dark eyes rolled. "At least give her the choice. Now will you go and find her? *Ask* her? Must I do *everything?*"

Jack laughed and slapped him on the shoulder. "You're a good friend, René. And a good man," he added, realizing both statements were not empty praise, but true.

"I know. I saved my country, the whole of France," he said, "with an infant monitor." He shrugged. "I am blessed with brilliance, what can I say? Adopt me."

The suggestion stunned Jack. For a moment he said nothing, then made a decision. "Unfortunately I can't do that, son, but I will sponsor you. Say the word. I'll see that you get a student visa and—"

René lowered his head and looked up from beneath his heavy lashes. A smile played around his mouth. "Jack, it was a joke. I have responsibilities here and an education to complete. My father has no one else to visit him in his isolated cell and I did make him a promise."

"You have seen him? How is he?" asked Jack.

"Lost to reality, but this is not a bad thing in his case, I think. I must stay." He stuck out his hand to shake. "But I will be your best man."

Jack shook his hand. "Thanks, René, but first I'll have to find a bride."

"I know. You are wasting time," René told him as he looked past Jack's shoulder. "She is waiting. Now you must excuse me. I have arrangements to make."

Jack turned and saw her. God, she looked so incredibly lovely. Silky hair swept across her brow and brushed the top of her shoulders. She moved with the fluid grace of a dancer. He remembered she had once considered ballet.

She wore pale yellow, the same shade of the blouse she had worn the first time he had seen her. This time it was a slip-like gown that shimmered over her slender curves like sunlight. It begged to be touched. His palms and fingers tingled with anticipation.

"Down, boy," he cautioned himself. "She's not yours yet."

And might never be. As if he had called out, Solange turned slightly, and their eyes met. She smiled and turned again, this time toward the glass doors that opened to the terrace.

Jack followed without even thinking, his gaze glued to the flow of her gown, the gleaming silk that brushed her shoulders, the pale, almost iridescent glow of her back.

Was she a fantasy? Had he really held this woman in his arms and loved her? Would he ever do so again?

She was facing him when he approached. The blue of her eyes seemed almost black in the dim lighting outside. She smiled up at him as his arms came around her. Her lips opened. *"Oui,"* she said, a mere breath of a word.

He kissed her deeply, soulfully, hoping to convey the richness of what she made him feel for her, how desperately he wanted her. When their lips parted, he gazed down at her. "Answer a question before it is asked and you take a big risk."

"You want to make love, that is in your eyes. My

answer is yes," she said, feathering her fingers through his hair.

"In my eyes, huh? I want you to marry me. That's what is in my heart," he said. "What's your answer to that?"

"Our time out of time is over, Jacques. This is the real world now with practical things to consider. I do not even know where you live or your favorite color or your middle name."

He kissed the tip of her nose. "Virginia, the blue of your eyes and Languedoc."

"Languedoc! Please say you are joking!" She laughed as he nodded. "Then I am sorry, but I must say no! Who could marry a man with a name like Languedoc?"

Jack grinned. "I'll change it." He hugged her. "My sunny girl, I think I have loved you from the minute I first saw you."

"Down the barrel of your weapon? Um, you did look interested."

"Absolutely smitten. I'm so glad you noticed."

"Will they need another doctor in Virginia, do you think?"

"*I* need you in Virginia, I *know*," he replied. "Seriously, will you? Will you marry me, Solange?"

She nodded. "Seriously, I will."

Applause interrupted the kiss. Jack broke it off, mildly annoyed that they had an audience, a little embarrassed by the state of his body and rocked off his foundation by the enthusiasm of their friends.

He kissed Solange's cheek, then muttered in her ear, "Where do we go in this mausoleum for a little privacy? If you expect me to wait until the wedding night, we'll have to marry right now."

She frowned up at him. "We cannot go up the stairs. They will see us and think us rude! Besides, they would know precisely *why* we were going, because there are only bedrooms."

"That's not a problem for me. I like bedrooms."

She ignored that, then brightened. "I know! We will lead everyone back inside for a toast. Then I will come back out this way, and in a moment or two, you will follow. Meet me in the garage in fifteen minutes," she said, smiling at the crowd who had followed them out, barely moving her lips as she spoke.

"The garage? I am *not* making love to my fiancée in a *car!*" he whispered. "There is no need for all this intrigue."

She drew back and frowned at him, pursing her lips provocatively, her blue eyes sparkling with deviltry. "And here you have led me to believe you lived for intrigue, that you were an adventurous spirit! A quarter hour or, as you Yanks would say, 'the deal is off.' What do you say to that, Mr. 008?"

He raised an eyebrow, loving this playful side of Solange. Hell, he loved every side of Solange. "I will consider it a mission."

Epilogue

"Honeymoon first is the only way to go," Jack declared. He trailed one finger over the swell of her breast and planted a kiss on the curve of her shoulder.

The wedding could not take place for ten whole days if they married in Paris. His documents could be faxed in a matter of hours, but there were strict civil laws and a ten-day wait that no amount of string pulling had been able to waive. They had decided to honeymoon in Venice while the banns were being called, since neither of them had ever been here.

She nuzzled the top of his head and lazily stroked his neck. "We should get out of the hotel and see the city. That *is* why we came here, after all."

"You, maybe," Jack said laughing. "I could care less about gondolas and the pigeons coating St. Mark's Piazza. This," he whispered, dragging a wet kiss along her neck, working his way down her lovely body, "is why I came."

Her laugh was low and sultry. "You promised me Venetian lace for my veil," she reminded him.

With a mock groan of surrender, he abandoned his quest and lay back against the pillows. "I guess I'll have to bribe you with souvenirs to get some cooperation here."

Again she laughed, turning to lie half on top of him. "I have *been* cooperating for the last forty-eight hours! Do you never tire?"

"Never." He grinned. "However, to tell the truth, I could use a good meal. Room service is beginning to pale and we have croissant crumbs in our bed."

"Someone is sure to ask for photographs when we go home," she warned him. "My camera is still packed away."

She was right. They had hardly seen anything since their arrival other than the dome of San Marco as they sailed the Grand Canal to the private dock of the Palazzo Sant Angelo Hotel. He had scarcely noticed the classical Venetian architecture of the ancient building or its elegantly appointed lobby. He had been too eager to have Solange alone at last.

She rolled from the bed naked and teased him with a provocative sashay across the room to the bath. "Join me?" she invited, entering the palatial enclosure lined with Carrara marble and containing an enormous sunken tub.

Ah, the memories they had made in that would stay with him a lifetime. He got up and followed to make more.

She reclined on the edge, fiddling with the taps, swishing in bubble bath as he devoured her with his eyes. Maybe he didn't need food after all.

"Will you mind so very much not having the others at the ceremony?" she asked. "Going through the civil one is more for my father and René than for me."

"The team and my family will attend the church wedding after we get home. That will be a fancier deal anyway."

She sat up and slid into the tub, swirling the water to froth it and smiling up at him. "And you must return to work soon after."

He sighed and nodded, not wanting to think about the job. He stepped into the bath with her, sat down and settled her on his lap. "The next assignment is already underway. Will is in place now."

"Holly must be so worried," she said with a sigh. "I must call her."

"Holly? What do you mean?"

"She loves him."

Jack shook his head but didn't bother setting her straight. It would serve no purpose at the moment to deflate her romantic notions. She was in love and wanted the world to be. Solange simply didn't yet understand the special relationship of his agents to each other.

He brushed off her notion and went on to briefly explain the mission. "We figure it will take at least two to three weeks before the rest of the team is needed for anything other than keeping tabs. Perhaps another few days to handle the aftermath. That will give you and my mother time to get to know each other and arrange the wedding. Dad can acquaint you with the hospital and get your accreditation underway. Before you know it, we'll be honeymooning again."

He smoothed a dangling curl off her brow, then reached for the soap.

She slid closer and embraced him. "Will the next mission be as dangerous for you as this last one?"

He cradled her, running his hands over the wet, satiny skin of her back. "Not for me, no. But, Solange, you know what I do. You will have to accept that I might be involved in something later that—"

"I understand," she said. "I would not change you, Jacques, any more than you would change me. I love who you are and what you are. Everything about you. 'Love is not love that alteration finds…'"

He smiled against her cheek and kissed it. "Okay, quote me poetry, then. Get me aroused and see what happens."

She turned her head and caught his lips with hers. The kiss was deep, soul shattering and sensual as hell. He forgot about missions and weddings and anything that existed outside that marble tub that held them.

She drew away and looked searchingly into his eyes. "You have taught me so much, Jacques." She threaded her fingers through his hair, her touch all about love and concern, her voice soft and whispery as French silk. "I know the enormous burden you have undertaken, the scope of what you do, the thousands of lives you save. This humbles me and yet it frightens me."

He cradled her face, cherishing the innocent, sweet earnestness he knew she would never lose. "And you, little doctor, have turned me inside out. Only a few weeks ago all I could see was the big picture and no faces. You blew my sense of detachment and isolation all to hell, you know. That's a little scary for me, too."

"You are no longer alone, Jacques," she promised.

On every level he was damned glad of that. The future of his world looked better than he could ever remember, and he had the one he adored right here in his arms.

* * * * *

Be sure to watch for Holly's romance,
UNDER THE GUN, coming only to
Silhouette Intimate Moments in late 2004.

Silhouette®

INTIMATE MOMENTS™

A new generation begins
the search for truth in...

A Cry in the Dark

(Silhouette Intimate Moments #1299)

by Jenna Mills

No one is alone....

Danielle Caldwell had left home to make a new life
for her young son. Then Alex's kidnapping rocked her
carefully ordered world. Warned not to call for help,
Dani felt her terror threatening to overwhelm her
senses—until tough FBI agent Liam Brooks arrived on
her doorstep, intent on helping her find Alex. Their
clandestine investigation led to a powerful attraction
and the healing of old wounds—and the discovery
of a conspiracy that could unlock the secrets of
Dani's troubled past.

The first book in the new continuity

FAMILY
SECRETS

THE NEXT GENERATION

Available June 2004 at your favorite retail outlet.

If you enjoyed what you just read,
then we've got an offer you can't resist!

Take 2 bestselling love stories FREE!
Plus get a FREE surprise gift!

Clip this page and mail it to Silhouette Reader Service™

IN U.S.A.
3010 Walden Ave.
P.O. Box 1867
Buffalo, N.Y. 14240-1867

IN CANADA
P.O. Box 609
Fort Erie, Ontario
L2A 5X3

YES! Please send me 2 free Silhouette Intimate Moments® novels and my free surprise gift. After receiving them, if I don't wish to receive anymore, I can return the shipping statement marked cancel. If I don't cancel, I will receive 6 brand-new novels every month, before they're available in stores! In the U.S.A., bill me at the bargain price of $3.99 plus 25¢ shipping and handling per book and applicable sales tax, if any*. In Canada, bill me at the bargain price of $4.74 plus 25¢ shipping and handling per book and applicable taxes**. That's the complete price and a savings of at least 10% off the cover prices—what a great deal! I understand that accepting the 2 free books and gift places me under no obligation ever to buy any books. I can always return a shipment and cancel at any time. Even if I never buy another book from Silhouette, the 2 free books and gift are mine to keep forever.

245 SDN DNUV
345 SDN DNUW

Name	(PLEASE PRINT)	
Address	Apt.#	
City	State/Prov.	Zip/Postal Code

* Terms and prices subject to change without notice. Sales tax applicable in N.Y.
** Canadian residents will be charged applicable provincial taxes and GST.
   All orders subject to approval. Offer limited to one per household and not valid to
   current Silhouette Intimate Moments® subscribers.
   ® are registered trademarks of Harlequin Books S.A., used under license.

INMOM02 ©1998 Harlequin Enterprises Limited